Searching for Candlestick Park

PEG KEHRET

PUFFIN BOOKS

PUFFIN BOOKS
Published by the Penguin Group
Penguin Putnam Books for Young Readers,
345 Hudson Street, New York, New York 10014, U.S.A.
Penguin Books Ltd, 27 Wrights Lane, London W8 5TZ, England
Penguin Books Australia Ltd, Ringwood, Victoria, Australia
Penguin Books Canada Ltd, 10 Alcorn Avenue, Toronto, Ontario, Canada M4V 3B2
Penguin Books (N.Z.) Ltd, 182-190 Wairau Road, Auckland 10, New Zealand

Penguin Books Ltd, Registered Offices: Harmondsworth, Middlesex, England

First published in the United States of America by Cobblehill Books,
an affiliate of Dutton Children's Books,
a division of Penguin Books USA Inc., 1997
Published by Puffin Books,
a member of Penguin Putnam Books for Young Readers, 1999

1 3 5 7 9 10 8 6 4 2

THE LIBRARY OF CONGRESS HAS CATALOGED THE COBBLEHILL EDITION AS FOLLOWS:
Kehret, Peg.
Searching for Candlestick Park / Peg Kehret.   p.   cm.
Summary: Determined to find his father and relive their good times,
twelve-year-old Spencer takes his cat, slips away from home in
Seattle, and sets out for Candlestick Park.
ISBN 0-525-65256-6 (hc.)
[1. Runaways—Fiction. 2. Cats—Fiction. 3. Fathers and sons—Fiction.] I. Title.
PZ7.K2518Se 1997 97-11222 [Fic]—dc21 CIP AC

Puffin Books ISBN 0-14-130366-2

Printed in the United States of America

For Mary Showers,
*my book list partner and founding member
of The Great Chicken Society*

Special thanks to:
Erin Karp,
my authority on bicycle routes;
Govind Karki,
for the personal tour of San Francisco;
and to
Pete and Molly,
for demonstrating cat behavior.

CHAPTER
ONE

I opened my eyes to darkness.

Mama's voice was low, and her hand shook my shoulder. "Spencer. Wake up!"

"What time is it?" I asked.

"It's two in the morning," Mama said.

I stuck my head under the pillow but Mama yanked the pillow right off again.

"Why are you waking me up at two o'clock in the morning?"

"You have to get up, Spencer. We're moving."

"Moving! Where are we going?"

"We'll stay at May's until we find a place. Hurry and pack your things." She dropped some paper bags on my bed.

"I'll pack in the morning," I said.

"You'll pack now. We need to be out of here before morning."

I sat up and looked around. In the light that leaked from the kitchen, I saw cardboard boxes and brown paper bags lining the hallway. Mama was serious. We really were moving out in the middle of the night.

"How come?" I asked.

"I don't have the rent money," Mama said. "I still owe for last month, and now it's due again. And they're coming tomorrow morning to repossess the car. We need to get moved before they take it."

Our being short of money wouldn't make headlines; Mama and I are *always* short of money. Mama's a waitress at Little Joe's, where most of the customers are not big tippers. We had a car taken back once before, and twice our electricity was shut off, but this was the first time we ever had to move because we couldn't pay the rent.

"As soon as I get a job, I'll pay part of the rent," I said. I was nearly thirteen, and I had my application in at three grocery stores. Sometimes kids are paid to retrieve shopping carts from around the parking lot and return them to the store. Ten cents a cart.

"We can't wait for you to grow up and find work. We're leaving here tonight."

"What about the furniture?" I asked.

"It isn't ours. Never has been. We rented this place already furnished; you know that."

2

I put on jeans and a T-shirt, and started stuffing the rest of my clothes in the paper bags. I could hear Mama in the kitchen, packing up her pans and the yellow dishes that used to belong to her mother.

Aunt May lived in the south end of Seattle. We lived in the north end, fifteen miles away. I was pretty sure I couldn't take the bus back here to school. I would have to go to school with my ten-year-old twin cousins, Buzz and Cissy, a prospect which did not thrill me.

Buzz and Cissy won't win any gold medals in the brains department and they scream and yell a lot, which gets on my nerves. Aunt May doesn't seem to mind, probably because she screams and yells a lot, too. I don't know if Buzz and Cissy's father screamed and yelled. He and Aunt May got divorced before the twins were born, and I don't remember him.

"When you're done in there, load your bags in the car," Mama said.

I picked up a sack of clothes and went out the kitchen door. The car was parked on the driveway that runs alongside the house; the back seat was already full of boxes. When I opened the trunk, the neighbor's Doberman, Bosso, started to bark.

"Hey, Bosso," I whispered. "It's only me." Bosso looks and sounds fierce but he knows me and always wags his stumpy tail when I talk to him through the fence.

An hour after Mama woke me up, everything was packed and loaded into the car. While Mama took

3

milk and eggs out of the refrigerator, I looked for Foxey.

I couldn't find him. I went through the house, looking under the beds and behind the furniture, in all the places he's ever hidden. No Foxey.

I always make sure he's in at night; usually he sleeps on my bed. He must have slipped out when Mama started loading the car.

I went into the backyard.

"Here, Foxey," I called. "Here, kitty, kitty, kitty."

"Quiet!" Mama said. "Do you want to wake up the whole neighborhood?"

"I can't find Foxey."

Mama put her bag of food in the car. "Let's go," she said.

"We can't leave without Foxey," I said. "I'll go out behind the garage and call him." My mouth felt dry. What if Foxey didn't come? I started toward the old garage that sits at the back of the property.

Mama rolled down her window. "Get in the car. We're leaving."

I knew Mama meant business about going right away. But I couldn't move out and leave Foxey behind. I just couldn't!

Foxey was a tiny kitten when I got him, three years ago. He has reddish brown fur and a bushy tail. I spent a long time choosing exactly the right name.

No matter what went wrong in my life, and there

had been plenty in the last couple of years, I could always count on Foxey to be glad to see me. When I had the flu, he jumped on my bed and purred. When I got a *D* in science because I refused to cut up a dead rat in class, Mama yelled and said I would never amount to a hill of beans, but Foxey jumped in my lap and kneaded his claws in and out, and I knew he would love me if I got all *D*s.

Every night I saved part of my dinner for him and he rubbed against my legs while I put it in his dish.

"You go on," I told Mama. "I'll stay until I find Foxey and then I'll take the bus to Aunt May's."

"We can't stay any longer because of that cat," Mama said. "May is waiting up to let us in and it's already later than I told her it would be."

I made one last desperate try. "Here, Foxey," I called. "Kitty, kitty, kitty."

Mama started the engine. "Get in this car," she said. "Now."

I knew that tone of voice. I got in.

"If you make me leave Foxey behind," I said, "I'll never forgive you. He won't know why I'm not here to take care of him. He'll starve to death."

"No, he won't. He's a good mouser."

"You could have told me sooner," I said. "I would have shut Foxey in the bathroom while we loaded the car."

"I had other things to worry about besides that fool

cat." She backed out of the driveway. "You probably couldn't keep a cat at May's house anyway. Cissy has a lot of allergies."

The truth is, Mama never liked Foxey much. She only let me keep him after I begged and cried and swore I'd always take care of him myself. I did, too. I fed him and combed him every day. Each month, I spent part of my lawn-mowing money on a new catnip mouse, the good kind from the pet store. Foxey loved his catnip mice.

I had bought him a cat collar, too, the stretchy kind that he could get out of if it ever got caught on something. I attached an identification tag with our phone number on it in case he ever got lost. That number won't help now, I realized. We don't live here anymore.

"Sometimes we have to do things we don't want to do," Mama said.

As we drove away from the house, I rolled down my window and looked back, still hoping to see a reddish brown cat with a bushy tail.

"Mrs. Ryan will probably adopt him," Mama said. "She likes cats."

I didn't answer. Mrs. Ryan lived next door. Her cat and Foxey sometimes fought with each other.

Mama kept talking. "You'll be busy at a new school, making new friends. Before you know it, you'll forget all about him."

She was wrong there. I knew I wouldn't forget Foxey. I would never forget Foxey. I would come back by myself and look for him. I would take the bus from Aunt May's house every day until I found Foxey and took him with me.

CHAPTER
TWO

I sneaked away the next night.

Aunt May's house is small, so the only place for me to sleep was on the couch. I waited until I was sure Mama and Aunt May and Buzz and Cissy were asleep. Then I got up and put on my clothes.

I took along one of the cardboard boxes that Mama had packed dishes in. I thought Foxey could ride in the box on the way back.

The buses don't run as often at night; I had to wait half an hour. It was spooky standing there alone so late at night but I was determined to go after Foxey.

It was nearly midnight when I got off the bus. As I walked toward our old house, I was surprised to see lights on in the house and a truck parked in the driveway. Had someone moved in already? If so, I hoped they hadn't let Foxey inside. He always went to the kitchen door and meowed when he wanted to go in. What if the new people had let him in? What if they thought he was going to be their cat? What if he was in there now? The curtains were closed so I couldn't see inside.

I walked quietly down the driveway, past the side of the house, into the backyard.

"Here, Foxey," I whispered. "Here, Foxey."

When I got to the back side of the house, I could see in. Two men were painting the kitchen. I wondered if they were the landlords that Mama owed the money to.

I couldn't see the floor, so I didn't know if Foxey was inside.

"Kitty, kitty, kitty," I said.

Bosso barked.

When Foxey didn't come, I decided to look in the garage. I pulled the garage door partway open.

"Here, Foxey."

From inside the garage, I heard, "Meow."

"Come, Foxey. Come on, you silly old cat." I peered into the darkness but I couldn't see him.

Because I was concentrating on Foxey, I didn't hear the back door of the house open.

"Hey! What are you doing out there?" The man's voice boomed out behind me.

I whirled around just as the porch light went on. The man stood on the porch step, looking at me.

I should have closed the garage door and told him who I was and what I wanted. Instead, I panicked. All I could think of was to get Foxey and beat it out of there as fast as I could.

I ducked inside the garage.

"I'm warning you!" the man yelled. "Get out of there."

Bosso barked louder and leaped against the fence.

I put my box on the floor, and flattened myself against the garage wall. Beads of sweat popped out on my upper lip.

I heard a soft *thud* as Foxey jumped down from the rafters. I knew the yelling had scared him. He tried to run out the door but I saw him in time and scooped him up.

"We called the cops," the man yelled.

The cops! I would be arrested for trespassing and get put in jail and Mama would be so mad she'd refuse to bail me out. I had to get out of there before the cops came. I decided to make a run for it.

I held Foxey tight against my chest and dashed out of the garage. I didn't stop to pick up the cardboard box.

The man started down the steps toward me.

I lunged sideways, reached over the top of the fence, and unlatched the gate. Bosso came snarling through, headed toward the man. Quickly, the man ran inside and slammed the door. Bosso followed him up the steps and stood at the top, barking.

I raced down the driveway, clutching Foxey. I didn't even look where I was going. I just ran. My feet pounded down the concrete driveway, then angled across the grass, and ran down the sidewalk.

Foxey's toenails dug into my shoulder but I couldn't stop. The cops would be there any second.

I wondered if the man had stayed inside or if he went straight through the house and out the front door. Maybe he was chasing me. I didn't look back to find out.

I ran.

When I got to the corner where the bus comes, I crouched behind a large, leafy bush, where I wouldn't be seen by any cars going past. If the landlord was looking for me, or if the cops came by, they wouldn't notice me there.

As I watched for the bus, I quickly regretted leaving the box behind; it was almost impossible to make Foxey stay with me. Bosso's barking had panicked him and now his cat brain had only one thought: ESCAPE!

He squirmed in my lap. He attempted to climb over my shoulder. He stuck his head under my arm and tried to squeeze through. I thought the bus would never come.

When it did, the driver wouldn't let me on. As I stepped off the curb, he said, "No animals allowed. Sorry."

"But I have to get home," I said, "and Foxey won't hurt anything. I'll hold him the whole time."

"Sorry, kid," the bus driver said. "Unless it's a Seeing-Eye dog, I'm not allowed to let an animal on the bus. I would lose my job."

I squeezed my eyes shut tight. "It's a Seeing-Eye cat," I said. "I'm blind and I'm participating in a special experiment with Seeing-Eye cats."

I heard the bus driver chuckle. Then I heard the bus door close.

As I opened my eyes, the bus pulled away from the curb.

Now what was I going to do? I couldn't walk all the way to Aunt May's house. And I sure couldn't afford a taxi.

I looked at the bus schedule on the signpost; it was half an hour until the next bus. That gave me plenty of time to think of a plan, and to get Foxey calmed down.

While I waited, I broke three-foot-long branches off the bush. By the time the bus arrived, I was ready.

As soon as I saw the bus approaching, I stuffed Foxey under my shirt. He made quite a lump. I pressed my left arm against my shirt to keep Foxey from squirming out. I laid the branches across the lump and held the stem ends with my left hand.

Luckily, it wasn't the same driver. This one gave me an odd look, as I dropped my quarters into the container and then folded my right arm across the branches, pushing them against my shirt.

"My mother makes dried flower arrangements," I said.

I walked quickly to the back of the bus and sat down. The driver watched me in the rearview mirror but he didn't say anything. I clutched Foxey close and hoped he wouldn't meow.

By the time I got to Aunt May's house, I was glad to put Foxey on the floor. My chest was covered with scratches. It wasn't Foxey's fault, though. He was scared. He had never ridden a bus before; it was noisy and he couldn't see where he was. Besides, he was hungry.

I cut up a hot dog and gave it to Foxey. While he ate, I put my pajamas on, and then I carried him to the living room. When I laid on the couch, he curled close beside me. The last thing I heard before I fell asleep was Foxey's purring.

Aunt May's scream jarred me awake. Nerves jangling, I sat up and looked to see what was wrong.

Aunt May and Mama stood beside me. They both had their hands on their hips. Aunt May glared at Foxey. Mama glared at me.

"How did that cat get here?" Mama demanded. "You answer me, Spencer Atwood. How did that fool cat get here?"

Foxey cowered under a chair, with his tail swishing from side to side.

"I won't have it," Aunt May said. "I have enough work without cat fur all over the house."

"I'll take care of him, Aunt May," I said. "He won't be any trouble for you."

"How did he get here?" Mama repeated.

"I've heard of cases," I said, "where a cat walked hundreds of miles and found its owner."

"Are you trying to make us believe that fool cat made its way clear across Seattle and found you?" Mama said.

"Foxey is very intelligent."

"Well, you aren't," Mama said, "if you think I'll buy that story. You sneaked out last night, didn't you? You went back to the old house and found that cat and brought him here."

"Yes, ma'am," I said. I figured I might as well admit it. I could see Mama wasn't going to let up until I did.

"Then you can take him right back," Aunt May said, "because he isn't staying here. Cissy's allergies might act up again."

"I can't take him back," I said. "There's no place to take him. Last night two men were painting the kitchen, and there was a big snarling dog on the back porch." I saw no reason to tell Mama that the big, snarling dog was Bosso.

Mama and Aunt May glanced at each other. Mama looked determined but I could tell Aunt May was weakening.

Just then Foxey came out from under the chair. He rubbed against Aunt May's ankles and purred. I knew Foxey was smart, but I didn't know he was that brilliant.

"If you can't take him back," Aunt May said, "you'll have to find a new home for him."

Foxey turned around and rubbed on her ankles again.

"He likes you, Aunt May," I said. "Usually he only does that to me, but he likes you."

"Don't you try to butter your aunt up, young man," Mama said.

Aunt May said, "He can stay here just until you find a home for him. Maybe it won't bother Cissy."

Mama threw up her hands. "You'll be sorry, May," she said. "Where's he going to find anyone silly enough to take that cat?"

"Thanks, Aunt May," I said. "I'll do extra chores, to make it up to you. I'll wash the dishes every night and weed your garden and . . ."

"You'll do that anyway," Mama said, "to repay May for letting us stay here. You have three days to find a home for the cat. Do you hear me, Spencer? Three days and then the cat goes to the Animal Control pound. And don't you sneak out at night again."

"Yes, ma'am." Three days. How was I going to find a home for Foxey in only three days?

I wasn't. Not in three days, not in three weeks, not in three years. I wasn't going to find a new home for Foxey, ever. Because I wasn't going to try.

On the morning of the third day, Mama said, "Have you found someone to take the cat?"

"Maybe," I said.

"No maybes. Did you find someone or didn't you?"

"A kid at school wants him."

"Fine. He can come get him this afternoon."

"He might not be able to come until Saturday." I was stalling, of course. No kids at school had said they wanted Foxey. How could they? Since I had no intention of giving him up, I had never mentioned him to anyone.

"If he wants the cat, he had better come today. Cissy had a sneezing attack last night and had to take her allergy pills."

"Maybe it wasn't Foxey's fault," I said. "Maybe she's allergic to Buzz."

"I know this is difficult for you," Mama said, "but if the cat is still here when I get home from work this afternoon, I'll have no choice but to turn it in to the pound."

I looked hard at Mama. I could tell that she meant it.

"Yes, ma'am," I said.

Mama isn't always so mean. I knew she was still angry at me for sneaking out to find Foxey.

"I'm working the breakfast and lunch shift," Mama said. "I'll be home at four o'clock."

"Foxey will be gone," I said. I did not add that I would be gone, too.

CHAPTER
THREE

✦

My mind galloped, trying to make plans. I knew I couldn't just run away. It's no good to run *away* from something. You have to run *to* something, or somewhere, or someone. But where could I go?

As if to say he was sorry for causing so much trouble, Foxey jumped in my lap. His purr rumbled out of his throat like a car whose engine idles too fast. I leaned down and scratched behind his ears, remembering back to that long ago day when I found a scrawny kitten cowering in the Target store parking lot.

"Dad!" I had said, pointing to the kitten. "Look!"

Dad liked animals, too, and he helped me calm the frightened kitten and carry it home.

When Mama saw it, she shook her head, no, but Dad said, "Oh, let the boy keep it," and eventually Mama gave in.

Dad moved out a few days later, so he had never seen how big Foxey got, and how beautiful.

Dad wasn't much for writing letters but sometimes I got postcards. The cards said things like, "Happy Birthday. I'll bet you're so big I wouldn't recognize you." They never told anything about himself.

Except for last time. The last one was postmarked June 15, San Francisco, and had a picture of Candlestick Park on it. Dad wrote, "Watch for me when the Giants are on TV. I'm here every day."

I showed the card to Mama. "He probably works for the Giants," I said. "Maybe he got hired as the batting instructor or the pitching coach."

"With no experience?" Mama said. "No coaching or playing, even in the minor leagues? Not likely."

I had to admit she was right about that.

Mama said, "Instead of buying baseball tickets, he should send support money."

I knew that wasn't likely, either, but I didn't say so.

Dad is not an ordinary, everyday baseball fan. Dad is a baseball nut. He played baseball in high school and if a broken wrist that failed to heal properly had not made him give up the sport, he would surely have gone on to play professional ball.

He would have played for the San Francisco Giants. It would not have mattered how much money another club offered him, Dad was a Giants fan, first, last and always.

Dad played center field and to hear him tell it, he was a center fielder right up there in quality with Willie Mays and Ken Griffey, Junior.

Mama always said, "Talk is cheap," when Dad started going on about his baseball skills, but I knew Dad wouldn't lie to me, not about something so important.

As I thought about Dad and that postcard, I knew where Foxey and I would go.

Mama put on her coat and started for the door. She said, "I'm sorry about the cat, Spencer, but this is May's house and I don't have any choice."

The spoonful of Wheaties stopped partway to my mouth. Those may be the last words you ever speak to your son, I thought, and my stomach felt twisted up like a pretzel.

"We can't be responsible for making Cissy sick," Mama added.

I felt like saying, "Why not? Cissy and Buzz make *me* sick," but I didn't want my last words to Mama to be fighting words, so instead I said, "You look pretty today, Mama."

"Sweet talk won't change my mind," Mama said. She picked up her purse, and hurried out to catch her bus.

I left for school as usual but instead of getting on the school bus with Buzz and Cissy, I told them that

I felt like walking that day and I took off by myself. I went around the block and quietly opened Aunt May's door.

When I stepped inside, I heard the shower running. Quickly, I went to the small table where Aunt May piles all of her real estate books, maps, fliers about houses for sale, and lists of potential customers. I took a map of Seattle and another that had Washington State on one side and Oregon on the other. Eventually, I would also need a map of California but I figured I would worry about that after I got close enough to need it.

After putting the maps in my backpack, I took Aunt May's purse out of the closet. I couldn't start on a long trip with empty pockets.

With my fingers on the purse's zipper, I hesitated. *This is stealing*, I thought. *For the first time in my life, I'm going to steal something.*

I closed my eyes, feeling guilty and ashamed. Even though I intended to repay her as soon as I could, it was wrong to take Aunt May's money.

But it would be wrong to leave Foxey at the pound, too. Foxey loves and trusts me. How could I abandon him to fear, and possibly death? That choice seemed even more wrong than taking money without permission. Money can be replaced; a living creature cannot.

I unzipped Aunt May's purse, and lifted out her wallet. Aunt May had sixteen dollars in cash. I took fourteen. I also took a little notebook and a pencil.

DISCARD

I replaced the wallet and the purse, and hurried into the kitchen, where Aunt May has a small desk. I found some envelopes and postage stamps and helped myself to one of each.

The shower stopped. I slipped out the back door, leaving it unlocked, and hid on the side of the house until I saw Aunt May go out the front door, get in her car, and drive away.

While I packed a few clothes and as much food as I could carry, I went over my plan. I would go to Candlestick Park and find Dad. There were still three weeks of baseball season left; I could get to San Francisco in three weeks, even if I had to walk the whole way.

Dad would be there; I was positive of that. He wouldn't leave when the Giants were still in the pennant race. Maybe Dad and I would go to the World Series together. Wouldn't that be something?

After I found Dad, Foxey and I would move in with him. Dad had been willing to let me have Foxey in the first place; he would let me keep him now. Foxey and I would live with him while I finished school. No more listening to Mama's complaints. No more worrying about money. No more moving out in the middle of the night. It would be wonderful.

I knew I had to leave Mama a note. If I didn't, she would worry herself into an early grave. Even though Mama got cranky, I never doubted that she loves me and I didn't want her thinking I had been kidnapped and hacked to pieces by an ax murderer. Outside of not having enough money, ax murderers are Mama's biggest concern.

I chose my words carefully.

> Dear Mama:
> I am on my way to Hollywood. Foxey is going to star in some cat-food commercials. I will let you know which channel to watch.
> Please do not try to find me. Do not worry about me; I will be careful.
> Your loving son,
> Spencer Atwood

This would throw Mama off track, since I had no idea in the world of going to Hollywood. I wasn't born yesterday; I know how hard it is to break into movies or television. Even though Foxey is the smartest and most handsome cat in the universe, it could take a few weeks to get him on a commercial.

Although I wasn't trekking to Hollywood on a wild cat chase, I figured if Mama thought I was in Hollywood, she would not be as likely to find me in San Francisco.

In my mind, I heard Mama's voice, loud and clear: "Thou shalt not tell a lie."

I left the note on the kitchen table.

I cut some air holes in a cardboard box. I wished I

had a regular cat carrier with a handle, but the box would have to do.

It wasn't too hard to get Foxey inside the box but the minute I put the cover on, and slipped rubber bands around it, he went berserk. He clawed at the inside of that box and yowled. He stuck his paws out through the air holes and scratched me. He thumped and jumped until the whole box rocked. I could see it was not going to be easy to carry Foxey all the way from Seattle to San Francisco.

I decided Foxey would have to learn to walk on a leash. I let him out of the box and he bolted under a bed while I cut an eight-foot length of Aunt May's clothesline rope. I tied one end around Foxey's collar and held on to the other end. It took him two seconds to wriggle his neck out of the stretchy collar.

Next I tied the rope around his middle but he thrashed and jumped like a fish on the line until I feared he would hurt himself.

There was a shopping center two blocks from Aunt May's house. I walked over there and bought a cat harness. It pained me to spend so much money but I could tell it was the only way I was going to get Foxey all the way to Candlestick Park. When I buckled the harness around Foxey, he flattened his ears and tried to bite it off.

"You'll get used to it," I told him.

I don't think he believed me.

While Foxey rolled on Aunt May's floor, trying to

escape from his harness, I looked at Aunt May's maps. There's no sense starting on a trip if you don't know which way to go.

I ran my finger down the map, through all the towns between Seattle and the California border. Olympia, Longview, Portland, Eugene, Medford. It wouldn't be an easy trip, especially on foot. And carrying a cat.

As I stared at the map, I wasn't sure I could make it in three weeks. I needed a faster way to travel.

"Foxey," I said, "we're going to take a train ride."

I knew where the trains stop because once, in the happy times, Dad took me to see the Seattle Mariners play baseball, and we saw a train at the King Street Station, right there next to the ballpark.

I double-checked my supplies, and added a bar of soap, a flashlight, and a small knife.

"Good-bye, Mama," I whispered, as I left Aunt May's house.

I waited at the bus stop until the first bus came along and then asked the driver how to get to the King Street Station. "Get in," he said. While I dropped my money in, he stared at Foxey's box, but he didn't ask me what was in it, and Foxey kept his mouth shut. Either he was all tuckered out or he had decided it didn't do any good to yowl and struggle.

I got off at the downtown bus tunnel and went up the steps. The King Street Station, an old brick building with a clock tower, was just across the street on my left. I crossed the street, which goes over the train tracks, and walked down the stairs into the station.

At the foot of the stairs, a vendor was selling popcorn, muffins, and other snacks. My stomach told me it was lunchtime, but I knew I couldn't afford to buy any food there; lunch would have to wait.

The large room with high ceilings held a feeling of anticipation. A line of travelers snaked away from a ticket counter. People with bags and boxes of belongings at their feet sat in rows of black chairs down the center of the room.

A lighted sign on the back wall announced arrivals and departures. I read the list, noting that trains went to Portland several times daily, including the train scheduled to depart next through Door #3. If I could sneak on board a train and ride to Portland, I would be 150 miles closer to San Francisco in just a few hours.

Door #3 was open. I walked out onto a small concrete area surrounded by a black wrought-iron fence. An opening in the fence faced the train tracks.

On the closest track, the Amtrak Superliner waited for passengers. The silver cars, each with a red and blue stripe, were higher than I expected. The door of the car closest to me was open; a yellow footstool stood below it, to help passengers step up into the train.

The open door of the Amtrak Superliner was only about thirty feet from where I stood. I swallowed hard and looked around. Two men, both wearing black pants, white shirts, and black vests, stood farther down the platform. One man held a clipboard and they studied the papers that were attached to it. Their backs were to me.

No other passengers had come outside. There was no conductor or ticket-taker, either. I could dash across the platform, step on the yellow stool, and be inside the train in only a few seconds. As long as the two men didn't turn around, no one would see me. Once I got on the train, I planned to hide in the bathroom until the train started moving. I had never ridden a train before, but I didn't think anyone would check the tickets again after we left the station.

Clutching Foxey's box in both hands, I sprinted toward the open door of the train. I had one foot on the stool and one foot on the bottom step of the Amtrak car when I heard, "Hey! You boy! What do you think you're doing?"

I looked over my shoulder and saw the two men in black vests running toward me.

"Get down from there," the taller one said.

I stepped back to the platform. "Isn't this the train to Portland?" I asked, hoping I didn't sound as scared as I felt.

"It is," the man replied, "but we aren't boarding yet."

"When will you be boarding?" I asked.

"Let me see your ticket," the other man said.

I made a show of feeling in my pockets before I said,

"I must have left it on the sink in the rest room." Then I hurried back through Door #3 into the station.

I went into the rest room, just in case the men were watching me. I washed my hands for a long time, while I waited for my breathing to return to normal. A few short hours ago, I had been an honest boy. Now I was a thief and a liar. I didn't like the way it made me feel.

When I came out of the rest room, I looked quickly around, afraid the men in black vests and a police officer might be waiting to question me. But the men had not followed me.

Even so, I wanted to get out of the train station. Instead of going up the stairs and leaving the station the way I had come, I quickly went out a door on the lower level.

At the corner of the station, I looked to my left and saw the train. The two men now stood on either side of the yellow stool like bookends.

Not wanting them to see me, I turned my back and walked away from the King Street Station. I was now in the Kingdome parking lot. It was nearly full of cars, and crowds of people hurried toward the gray dome-shaped stadium. Many wore blue Mariners' baseball caps. I realized the Seattle Mariners were playing an afternoon baseball game. Logos on T-shirts and sweatshirts said, REFUSE TO LOSE and MARINER MAGIC. Some fans carried bags of peanuts or seat cushions.

A boy about my age hurried along with his dad. He

had a baseball glove on his left hand. They were laughing, and the man took two tickets out of his shirt pocket and handed one of them to the boy.

A terrible yearning tore at my insides. I stood still and watched until the boy and his dad were out of sight.

Soon, I told myself, that will be me and Dad, going into Candlestick Park to watch the Giants. Soon. If the train wasn't possible, I would get to Candlestick Park some other way.

Foxey scratched at the inside of the box, trying to dig a hole in the bottom. Before long, I would need to let him out to stretch. I hurried away from the stadium, passed the bus tunnel, and walked along the sidewalk.

This section of Seattle is called the International District; I peered into small shops that sell exotic pastries and colorful clothing. If people can immigrate to the United States all the way from China and Viet Nam, I thought, I can surely find my way from Seattle to San Francisco.

Three boys passed me on bicycles, talking a language I couldn't understand. I watched as they stopped their bikes in front of a grocery. Wooden stands full of bananas, mangoes, oranges and kiwis lined the sidewalk outside the grocery.

None of the boys locked their bikes. They just rested the handlebars against the fruit stands and went inside the store.

My eyes swept quickly across the three bikes. I chose the blue one because it had a flat place over the back wheel—perfect for Foxey's box to ride on.

As I made this decision, I heard Mama and Aunt May, in unison, telling me, "Thou shalt not steal," but I closed my ears to their imagined sermons, ran forward, and grabbed the blue bike.

With Foxey's box under one arm, I pushed off, pedaling as hard as I could. I was all the way to the corner before a trio of voices shouted behind me.

CHAPTER
FOUR

I skidded around the corner, leaped off the bike, and dragged it into the lobby of a sleazy-looking hotel. I laid the bike on the floor, where it wouldn't show through the front window.

I went to the hotel counter, past three whiskery men who looked as if they'd been sitting in the lobby so long they'd put down roots. They stared blankly at me, and I tried to appear casual, though my heart was thundering in my ears.

The bored man behind the counter glanced away from a TV set and narrowed his eyes at me suspiciously.

"How much does a room cost?" I asked.

"You alone?"

"Yes." I didn't mention Foxey, since I would not be renting a room anyway. I stood sideways at the counter so I could see out the front window while we talked.

"Eleven dollars. Cash in advance. One bed; bathroom at the end of the hall."

I pretended to count my money while I watched the window. The three boys—two on bicycles and one trailing them on foot—raced past. Slowly, I put my money back in my pocket. When the boys did not return, I thanked the clerk, and said I could not afford a room.

As I bent to pick up the bike, I looked out the window. Seeing no sign of the three boys, I pushed the bike out of the hotel and rode away fast.

I knew which direction was west because that's where the water is. If you go west in Seattle, you eventually wind up at Elliot Bay, a part of the water of Puget Sound. From that I could figure out which way was south, and I headed south.

All I cared was that I was going in the right direction. I didn't have enough time or money or leg muscle to go out of my way. It isn't easy to ride a bike one-handed and hold a box full of cat under the other arm.

When I'd ridden twenty minutes with no sign of the boys or a police car coming after me, I stopped and opened the box. I tied one end of the rope to Foxey's harness and wrapped the other end around my wrist, to be sure he wouldn't pull it out of my hand.

While Foxey slunk around on the sidewalk, I poked

two holes in the bottom of the box. I cut a piece of the rope, threaded the ends through the holes from the inside, and tied the box to the platform on the bicycle. I would make a lot better time with both hands on the handlebars.

When the box was secured, I gave Foxey a small piece of cheese. I opened the peanut butter jar full of water that I'd put in my backpack, and poured a little in the lid. He dipped his nose in it, but didn't drink any.

Last, I encouraged him to use a patch of dirt for his bathroom. He was too nervous, though, so I put him back in his box, secured it with the rubber bands, and took off again.

It felt good to ride along on the bicycle, with the wind blowing against my face. I wondered how many miles I could make in a day if I pedaled from the time the sun rose until it set, stopping only to eat, and to exercise Foxey.

I began to think ahead, to daydream about actually walking into Candlestick Park and circling through the stands, looking for Dad. I imagined his joy when he saw me. I thought how he would hug me and take me home with him after the game and tell me how much he had missed me, especially in the summer, on Saturday afternoons.

Dad and I used to watch a baseball game together every Saturday at one o'clock. It was a small thing, really. Not like having a dad who actually did stuff with you, such as playing catch, or going hiking, or making projects out of wood.

Watching TV together is probably not what the child psychology books suggest on how to create a loving relationship with your kid. Still, Dad and I always looked forward to Saturday afternoon. We'd make a big bowl of popcorn and Mama would leave us alone as we cheered and booed and discussed the plays. On summer Saturdays, Dad and I had something in common.

The first Saturday after he left, I thought for sure he'd be back. Mama had told me when he left that he would not be living with us anymore, but I expected him to visit me on Saturday afternoons.

It's up to them whether they can get along together or not, and if they don't love each other anymore, I can't do anything about it. But just because Dad left Mama, that doesn't mean he had to leave me, too, does it?

That may sound childish for a nine-year-old, which is what I was when he left, but it's how my thinking went that first week. Probably I was a little out of my noggin, as Aunt May says, which means I was half nuts and not thinking any too clearly.

It sounds dumb now, but I truly expected him to come home that first Saturday—just long enough to watch the Game of the Week with me. I knew he wouldn't *stay*. I knew he and Mama were really through. But I made the popcorn and tuned in the set and stood by the window, watching for his car.

"He won't be here," Mama said. "Do you want me to play cards with you?"

"It's Saturday. Dad and I always watch the baseball game together."

"Not anymore," Mama said. "I'm sorry."

Not anymore. She didn't say, "Not this week," or "Not for awhile." She said, "Not anymore," and I knew she meant forever.

When Dad didn't come back that first Saturday, I turned off the TV in the fifth inning and never watched baseball again. Not even the World Series.

Well, I could get back into it easily enough. Once Foxey and I were living with Dad, I would look forward to Saturday afternoons again, instead of dreading them as I had for the last three years.

I pedaled along. Visions of Dad and me sharing popcorn and yelling for the Giants filled my head. I didn't see the rock in the road until my front tire hit it. The bike swerved sideways. The back tire scraped against the curb, and the bike toppled.

I flew over the handlebars and dropped toward the street. I flung my left arm across the top of my head, with my hand on my right ear. There's a law in Washington State that you have to wear a protective helmet when you ride a bicycle, but the kid I stole the bike from still had the helmet on his own head so I had to rely on my arm to save me from a fractured skull or a concussion or any of the other bad things that can happen to an unprotected head.

It turned out it wasn't my head that needed protection; it was my right leg. My shin, just above the ankle, smashed into the curb as I went down. Pain zapped up to my knee and down to my toes like bolts of electricity, bringing tears to my eyes.

I was afraid I had broken my leg or, at the very least, chipped a bone.

I reached for the box, which was still tied to the back of the bike, and stuck my finger in one of the air holes.

"Are you okay, Foxey?" I asked.

Foxey was quiet.

I sat up, feeling woozy, and opened the box. Foxey was flattened in the bottom with his ears back. His eyes were huge. I ran my hands over him, digging my fingers into his fur. He didn't yowl or hiss or try to get away, so I guessed he wasn't hurt.

A car stopped and a woman in a green jogging suit got out and hurried over to me. I clamped the top back on the box and slid the rubber bands in place.

"Are you all right?" she asked. "Should I call 911?"

"I'm scraped up, that's all." If I told her the truth, that my leg felt as if I'd just been whacked with a baseball bat, she would call 911 for sure, and they would call Mama, and instead of spending the night in Tacoma, as I planned, I'd be back on Aunt May's couch. And Foxey would be in a cage at the pound, starting the countdown.

"Can you stand up?"

I clenched my teeth and struggled to my feet. When I stood, the blood rushed downward; my leg throbbed. I put all my weight on the other foot.

"I'm just a little sore," I said. "Nothing serious."

"What's your name?" she asked. "I have a cellular phone in my car. If you give me your name and a phone number, I can call your family and have someone come to get you."

"Nobody's home," I said. "They're at work."

"Give me your mother's work number."

"You don't need to call anybody," I said. "I'm really okay. And I only live a couple of blocks from here. I'll push my bike home and then I'll rest until Mama gets there."

The lies rolled off my tongue so quickly that I wondered if lying is one of those skills where the more you do it, the better you get. Like practicing the trumpet.

"You're sure? You look pale. I'd be glad to drive you home. The bike won't fit in my car, but someone could come and get it later."

"Thanks anyway," I said. "I don't want to leave my bike. Someone might steal it." Silently I added: It's already been stolen once today.

She hesitated a moment and then started back to her car.

"Thanks for stopping," I said. "It was nice of you."

"You're welcome." She got in, and drove away. As I watched her leave, I wondered if I was making a big mistake by not accepting her help. What if I really did need a doctor?

I pushed the bike a few feet, just in case she was watching me in her rearview mirror. When she turned at the next corner, I flopped down on the curb. I pulled my pants' leg up and examined my shin. There was a lump the size of a lemon, just above my ankle. It was already turning black and blue, but it didn't hurt quite as much as before.

I squeezed the swollen area gently, the way Mama tests tomatoes at the supermarket, and then exhaled with relief. I was pretty sure nothing was broken.

If I were home, Mama would put ice cubes in a plastic bag and set the bag on my leg. She'd have me lie down, with a pillow under my foot, and bring me a glass of orange juice. "Drink it all," she would say. "Vitamin C helps a body heal."

I thought how wonderful it would feel to stretch out on Aunt May's couch with my foot up, and let Mama fuss over me. She might even bring my dinner on a tray.

But Mama would also tell me that I could not go to San Francisco to live with Dad. No way. No time. No how.

And Aunt May would look at my bruised leg and say God was punishing me for stealing.

I mounted the bike and started pedaling. Every time I pushed my right foot down, pain climbed my leg. I tried to push harder with my left foot and go easy on the right. It hurt like crazy, but my other option was to sit on the curb all night.

I left the industrial area, and saw apartments and houses.

When I came to a small park, I decided to spend the night there. I had hoped to get farther, but my leg hurt badly and Foxey had started yowling again, and the park looked as safe a spot as I was likely to find. There was a children's play area, with swings and slides, several picnic tables, and a rest room, which I needed to use.

The park was empty, which suited me just fine. I wasn't exactly sure what Mama would do when she found my note, but she might call the police and report me missing. My description might be on the evening news, and Buzz and Cissy might nail MISSING posters, with my picture, on all the telephone poles.

I may not be the child genius of the world, but I could figure out that the fewer people who noticed me, the less likely it would be that one of them would turn me in.

The woman who had stopped to help me when I fell off the bike would recognize my picture if she saw it on television. The clerk in the hotel might, too. And the two Amtrak conductors. Already four people could identify me, and this was only my first night away from home. I would have to be more careful.

I put Foxey's box on a picnic table, and opened the lid. He raised his head cautiously, sniffing the air while I tied the rope on his harness. He stepped out of the box and sat on the picnic table for a couple of minutes, looking all around. Then he stretched, first his front legs and then his back legs.

I watched carefully, still worried that he might have been injured in the bike accident. He jumped from the table to the bench to the ground and examined the underside of the bench. I decided he was okay, and turned my attention to food.

I ate an apple, two slices of bread, and a piece of cheese. I gave Foxey some cheese, too. I offered him a bite of bread and he surprised me by eating it. I wished I had a cold glass of milk.

Foxey began to explore. I let him go where he wanted and I followed, holding the rope. He walked slowly, stopping often to check behind him.

Once he ate a big bite of grass. I had seen him do that at home, too. I guess cats need salad, the same as people do. Mama always told me to eat my greens.

Mounds of dirt, where moles had tunneled to the surface, dotted the park's grassy area. Foxey approached a molehill cautiously, and sniffed the dirt. Then he began to dig, pushing the fresh dirt away with both paws.

I thought he smelled the mole and was trying to get

it. I clutched the rope, ready to pull him away if a mole jumped out. Moles have razor-sharp claws, and I didn't want a slashed cat on my hands.

Foxey dug faster and faster, and then stepped forward and squatted over the hole. I laughed, hoping the moles either had an umbrella or were in a different part of their tunnel. When he finished, Foxey carefully scratched the dirt back into place and continued his walk.

After awhile, Foxey quit walking and just sat, so I carried him back to the picnic table. "If you're going to sit still," I told him, "you can do it where I have a place to write."

Foxey lay in the grass and I got out the small notebook that I had found in Aunt May's purse. The first page was a grocery list, which I tore out. The rest of the pages were blank. I wrote: SPENCER'S DEBTS. On the next page I wrote:

1. Aunt May $14

> *one small notebook*
> *one stamped envelope*
> *bread, apples, cheese, graham crackers*
> *rope; knife, soap, flashlight*
> *maps*

2. Unknown boy: Bicycle

I had not yet thought of any way to get the bike back to its owner. If I took it to the Seattle police, they'd want to know how I got it. Still, I knew I had to repay that debt somehow.

When I had recorded my debts, I put Foxey under one arm, and walked the bike over to the rest room. Shrubs grew all around the building. I decided to sleep next to the shrubs, where I wasn't likely to be noticed by anyone going down the street past the park at night. I found a secluded spot between two bushes on the back side of the building, and prepared to spend the night.

I didn't have a blanket, but I did have a sweatshirt and a stocking hat. I put both of them on, for September nights get chilly. I decided to let Foxey be out of the box overnight. With one end of the rope tied to Foxey's harness and the other end tied securely around my wrist, I lay down on the ground.

I was glad I had the notebook, to keep track of what I owed. Somehow writing it all down made it official that I was not a thief; I was a person who temporarily needed to borrow from someone else. If an ax murderer got me before I found Dad, the police would find my debt notebook on my body and give it to Mama, and she would know her son was honest to the end.

Thinking about ax murderers did not help me fall asleep.

FIVE

Darkness settled around me. On the far side of the park, lights went on in windows, and I wondered about the people who lived in those houses. Were they eating dinner? Watching the news? Reading to their kids? I wondered what Mama was doing.

When I was little, Mama used to make up stories for me, with heroes named Spencer. No, I told myself. Don't think about the past. Think about the future instead. I squeezed my eyes shut tight and imagined I was sitting in Candlestick Park with Dad, watching the Giants play baseball.

I fell asleep, jerked awake, and fell asleep again. Sometime in the night, Foxey growled. My eyes flew open. Instantly, every nerve in my body was alert. What had he heard?

Foxey was crouched beside my left shoulder, his tail swishing nervously back and forth, brushing against my cheek. I lay still, listening. I was afraid to sit up and look, for fear whoever or whatever was there would hear me move.

I inched my right hand across my chest and stroked Foxey, hoping to soothe him. He growled again.

Clink. Clink. Clink. I recognized the sound of a dog's tags jingling together. Foxey stood up and arched his back. Even in the dark, I could tell his fur was standing out, making him twice his regular size.

Clink. Clink. Clink. The sound came closer.

I sat up. I couldn't see the dog through the bushes.

I reached for Foxey's box, and opened it. If the dog spotted us, I thought it would be safer for Foxey to be in the box. A dog might not even come to investigate a boy with a box but it would go after a cat, for sure.

I untied the rope from my wrist and then reached for Foxey. I planned to put him in the box and put the box behind me. If the dog approached, I would not let it see the box.

Foxey struggled when I picked him up, and let out a loud, "Meow," when I put him in the box. The dog immediately crashed through the bushes toward us, barking.

Foxey panicked. Before I could clap the lid on the box, he leaped out of my grasp and streaked around the end of the rest room. I still had the rope in my hand, with the other end attached to Foxey's collar, but the dog saw Foxey go, and bolted after him.

I jumped to my feet, which made my right leg throb.

I had to make a fast choice. I could hold onto the rope and keep Foxey from running away, but if I did that I knew the dog would reach Foxey before I could pick him up. Or I could let go of the rope, and hope Foxey would be able to run fast enough to get away from the dog. If he did, where would he go? Would I be able to find him again?

I let go.

I had to. I was afraid if I held Foxey back, the dog would tear him to pieces before I could get there.

Woof. Woof. Woof. As the end of the rope slid out of my hand, the barking was loud and excited.

The dog chased Foxey, and I ran after the dog. "Go away!" I yelled. "Get out of here, dog." I clapped my hands. "Shoo!" I cried. "Go home!"

The barking grew more high-pitched. I followed it around the rest room. As soon as I got away from the bushes, I could see that it was a big dog—a German shepherd, perhaps, or some kind of a setter. I hoped it wasn't a trained hunting dog.

We dashed across the grassy field in the center of the park: Foxey first, the dog gaining on him, and me limping after. Every time my right foot thumped down, I felt a jolt of pain up my leg.

Woof! Woof!

The dog suddenly stopped running, but kept barking. Did he have Foxey cornered? Had Foxey made a mistake and gone somewhere that he couldn't get out of? I pushed myself to run faster. "Hey, dog!" I yelled, hoping to distract it.

The barking grew louder.

As I got closer I saw that the dog was standing at the base of a tree, barking upward into the branches. Good old Foxey had climbed a tree. The dog stood on its hind legs, with its front paws on the tree trunk, still barking.

"Go home, dog," I said. "Stop that!" I didn't raise my hand or go close to the dog, though. I like dogs, but I didn't know anything about this one, and I didn't want it to come after me.

The dog leaped against the tree trunk, barking shrilly.

A porch light came on across the street, at one of the houses I had seen earlier.

A woman in a blue bathrobe stepped out onto an open porch. "Here, Peppy!" she called. "Here, Peppy!"

The dog stopped barking and turned to look at her.

"Peppy!" the woman yelled. "Come home!"

The dog circled the tree again, nose to the ground.

The woman quit calling and started to whistle.

The dog looked up into the branches one last time, and then trotted toward the woman. I waited until I saw her let the dog in and close the door before I went to the base of the tree. I walked around it, hoping the rope would dangle down far enough for me to grab it. I knew I couldn't haul Foxey out of the tree that way, but at least if I held the end, I would eventually be able to get Foxey back. I didn't see any rope.

"It's okay, Foxey," I said. "He's gone. You can come down now."

I don't think Foxey believed me. I stared up into the dark branches. There was no sound, and no movement.

"Here, kitty, kitty. Come on, Foxey." Nothing.

My flashlight was on the ground next to the bicycle; I wished I had grabbed it before I ran after the dog. Now I didn't want to leave the tree to go get the flashlight, because I was afraid Foxey might jump down while I was on the other side of the park and who knows which direction he might go. I decided to wait at the base of the tree, and hope he would come to me.

I sat on the ground, leaned back against the tree, and waited. After a few minutes I called him again. No response. Poor Foxey, I thought. He's terrified, and I don't blame him.

Maybe I wasn't being fair to Foxey, taking him with me on this trip. Maybe I should have done what Mama said, and tried to find him a good home. If I had showed his picture around school, lots of people would have wanted such a beautiful, smart cat. Some rich kid might have adopted him and Foxey would be sleeping on a heated pillow and eating tuna out of a glass bowl, instead of shaking with fear at the top of a tree.

"I'm sorry, Foxey," I said.

I waited and called, waited and called, for about an hour. Then a new worry hit me. What if Foxey wasn't in the tree? The dog could have made a mistake. I never actually saw Foxey go up the tree; I only saw the dog barking at the bottom. Foxey might have run partway up, to fool the dog, and then run right down the other side and kept going. By now, my cat could be miles away, still running.

I stood up, called one more time, and then jogged across the park, to get the flashlight. All this running wasn't doing my sore leg any good, but I was more worried about Foxey than I was about my leg. I grabbed the flashlight, and ran back to the tree.

I turned on the light and aimed it into the branches, waving it back and forth. I looked at the large lower branches first, and them aimed the light higher and higher. Nearly at the top, two green eyes gleamed in the light.

"Silly old cat," I said, as relief filled me. "Come down from there."

He lay on his stomach, his front paws extended in front of him, holding onto the branch. The rope was tangled in the branches below him; it was probably the reason Foxey wasn't higher than he was. He couldn't keep climbing because the rope held him back. Was it also keeping him from climbing down? If it was, I had a serious problem.

I turned off the flashlight, not wanting to call attention to myself. Now that I knew where Foxey was, I decided to wait awhile longer and see if he could get down by himself.

I sat against the tree again, and waited. My eyelids kept closing and twice I had to stand up and walk around the tree to keep myself from falling asleep.

I tried talking softly to Foxey, encouraging him to come down. After about forty-five minutes, I turned on the flashlight. Foxey now faced the opposite direction, with his head toward the tree trunk. But he wasn't any lower.

I squinted upward, trying to see if the rope was the problem. I couldn't tell.

Once when he was still a kitten, Foxey had gone up our neighbor's chestnut tree and I had been afraid he didn't know how to climb down. I wanted to call the fire department, but Mama said, "If the cat got up there alone, he'll get down alone." Dad said, "Don't worry, Spencer. I've never seen a cat skeleton hanging in a tree."

They were right. Foxey came down the next morning, but not until I had skipped supper and breakfast because I was too upset to eat.

This time, I couldn't wait until morning. Once daylight came, I didn't dare hang around this tree too long without someone wondering who I was and why I was not in school. And I couldn't leave the tree and take a chance that Foxey would jump down and run away. Besides, Peppy's owner would no doubt let him out again first thing in the morning, and he would probably beeline right over here.

I stuffed the flashlight in my hip pocket, and walked to the closest picnic table. I pulled on the table, hoping it wasn't chained to a pole or cemented to the ground.

It moved. I yanked harder. It took all my strength to drag the picnic table across the grass. After I pushed one end of the table against the base of Foxey's tree, I crouched under that end and stood up. My back helped my arms lift the heavy table and I leaned the raised end against the tree, centering the table on the tree trunk so the table wouldn't wobble.

When it was as steady as I could make it, I climbed up the tabletop, the way little kids climb up the slope of a slide. Then I stood on the top end of the table, and stretched my arms above my head until I grasped the bottom branch of the tree. I pulled myself up, scraping both arms on the bark, and sat on the branch.

I shined the light on Foxey again. He had not moved.

I held the light against my chest so that it illuminated my face. I wanted to be sure Foxey knew it was me coming up the tree.

"Good boy," I told him. "Good Foxey. You can come down now."

I turned the light off, put it back in my pocket, and stood up, holding fast to the next branch up. It was three feet above the one I was on; I climbed up to it easily. From there on up the branches got smaller, with short branches sticking out from the main ones. I kept climbing.

"Meow."

Foxey was only about six feet above my head when he greeted me. I was afraid to go any higher. The branches were thin up this high and I wasn't sure they would support my weight.

I talked to Foxey some more. He meowed again, but didn't move.

I took the flashlight out of my pocket and turned it on. I could now reach the end of the rope and, holding the flashlight under one arm, I began untangling it. Twice I had to break off a small branch in order to free up the rope. When I finally had it all loose, I tugged gently, urging Foxey to come down toward me.

Foxey scowled at me and stayed where he was.

I tugged again. On the third try, Foxey stood up, stretched, and hopped down to the branch next to my shoulder. I scooped him off the branch, held him against my chest, and buried my face in his fur.

After putting the flashlight in my pocket, I backed down the tree, holding Foxey with one hand and hanging onto branches with the other.

When I reached the bottom branch I sat down and

let my legs dangle over. I could see the ground, but it was too far to jump, especially with my sore leg.

I wasn't sure I could climb from the branch to the picnic table and hold onto Foxey at the same time. I decided to let Foxey go first. I tied the end of the rope around my wrist and, holding Foxey with both hands, I leaned over as far as I could toward the picnic table, and let go.

Foxey landed with a light thud and scampered down the table to the ground. As he did, I hung from the branch and jumped, feeling for the table with my feet. They landed too far to one side, and the table tilted away from the tree trunk.

Instead of sliding down the table, as I had planned, I jumped forward as the table crashed sideways to the ground. I landed on my hands and knees in the grass.

The noise and sudden movement startled Foxey and he bolted away. The rope yanked on my wrist, as Foxey thrashed wildly at the other end.

I scrambled to my feet and ran toward him, but as soon as there was slack in the rope, he took off again.

Fortunately, he ran toward the bushes beside the rest room, and when I reached the building, I reeled him in like a fish, picked him up, and held him close. I felt his heart thumping.

"I'm sorry, Foxey," I whispered. "I'm sorry you got so scared."

After he quieted down, I settled into the spot where I had been asleep earlier. This time I put Foxey in the box; I thought he might feel safer that way. I didn't put the lid on, though, since the rope was still tied to us both. I lay on my side, curled around the box, petting Foxey.

It took me a long time to fall asleep. I kept listening for the jingle of dog tags.

SIX

I awoke at dawn with a stiff neck. It took me a second to remember where I was. As soon as I did, I looked in Foxey's box. It was empty.

I sat up, and saw him under a bush, watching a bird.

"How about some breakfast?" I said, as I opened the backpack. We shared bread and cheese, and I ate one of Aunt May's apples. After a walk around the park, during which Foxey made good use of another molehill, I tied the box to the bike, put him in, and started on our way.

Although my leg still hurt, I peddled the bike at full speed, using both legs equally. There were a lot of cars on the streets, but the drivers paid no attention to me.

They were no doubt on their way to work and thought I was on my way to school.

At noon, I stopped at a Plaid Pantry and bought a box of cat food ($1.69), a quart of milk ($1.10), and two Rice Krispies cookies ($1.50). Mama says you pay more at a convenience store, but I didn't want to leave Foxey out of my sight while I walked through a big supermarket. At Plaid Pantry, I could see my bike through the front window the whole time.

I sat on the sidewalk in front of a French restaurant that didn't open until three, and ate the last of my bread and drank the milk. I ate one cookie and saved one for later. Then I counted my money.

Yesterday morning, I had sixteen dollars and seventy-five cents. Fourteen dollars came from Aunt May's purse; the rest was left from my lawn-mowing money. Foxey's harness cost $3.20, and the bus to the King Street Station was seventy-five cents, so I had actually left Seattle with $12.80 in my pocket. Now I had only $8.51.

I put some cat food in Foxey's box, but the traffic noise made him too nervous to eat. I poured the last bit of milk into the jar lid and put it in the box. While Foxey drank the milk, I studied the Washington map. I knew I couldn't ride my bike on the freeway; I had to find other roads.

As the day wore on, my leg hurt more. After lunch, I rode for only an hour and then I had to rest. The second time I stopped, I was near an on-ramp for Interstate Five.

I stood near the freeway on-ramp, watching the cars approach. A traffic light controlled when the next car could merge, and a line of cars waited. It would be easy to hitchhike from here, I thought. Each car stopped briefly at the light; they were heading south, the way I needed to go. Maybe I should just go out on the side of the road and stick my thumb in the air.

The thought of hitching a ride scared me silly. What if I got picked up by a criminal or a drunken driver?

On the other hand, I would get to California a lot faster in a car, and without wrecking my leg. My bruised shin hurt more now than it had when I first fell. All the bike riding was making it worse.

I did some quick calculations. If a car went sixty miles an hour for four hours, and I was in it, I'd be 240 miles closer to Candlestick Park by dinnertime.

I stepped closer to the curb, looking at the vehicles in the line. I needed a big car, so that my bike would fit. And I needed a driver who did not look as if he had a police record.

The fourth car back seemed perfect: it was a full-size van, with a white-haired woman behind the wheel and a little kid in the front seat. Grandma and grandchild, I guessed. The back seat was down; my bike would fit easily.

I waited until the van was second from the stoplight. Then I put out my thumb.

The woman noticed me right away, and rolled down her window. I couldn't believe my good fortune. The first one I tried was going to give me a ride.

But instead of telling me to get in, the woman started yelling at me.

"Does your mother know what you're doing?" she shouted. "It isn't safe to hitchhike, and it isn't legal, either. What's your name? Where do you live?"

The control light turned green. The pickup truck behind the van honked. "You go home this minute!" the woman called, as she drove onto the freeway.

The pickup honked again, and I realized he was not honking at the van; he was honking at me. The driver was a man in a red baseball cap. He jerked his hand toward the back of the truck, signaling me to hop in.

There wasn't time to think it over. It was do it, or get left. I hoisted the bike into the back of the truck, and climbed up beside it. As the truck picked up speed, I untied the box from the bike, and held it on my lap so Foxey wouldn't be riding along tipped on his side.

I scooted forward until my back rested against the cab. I wondered if the woman was right, that it's against the law to hitchhike.

Foxey meowed, letting me know he wanted to get out of the box.

"Sorry," I told him. "You're safer where you are."

But am I safe? I wondered. Was this a smart move or the most stupid thing I'd ever done?

I looked over my shoulder, through the window, at the driver. His chin had not been near a razor for several days. His T-shirt sleeves were rolled up and I saw a large tattoo of a dragon on the arm nearest me. Aunt May would take one look and scream. Mama would say he has an ax under the seat, for sure.

What if Mama was right? I had put out my thumb for the grandma in the van, not for this man; why had I been so quick to hop in his truck?

I decided that the minute the truck got off the freeway and stopped, I would jump down and take off on the bike. But what if he didn't stop until he was in some remote area? I began to envision a cabin in the wilderness, where kids are tortured.

Twenty minutes later, the truck slowed. As it exited the freeway, I quickly tied Foxey's box back on the bike and slid over to the tailgate, ready to make my getaway. The driver turned at the first corner, pulled over, and stopped.

I jumped down and opened the tailgate. Before I could get the bike off, the man came around to the back of the truck. I wanted to run, but I couldn't leave Foxey.

"This is as far as I go," the man said, as he helped me lift the bike to the ground. "Good luck."

"Thanks," I said. I took a deep breath, and felt my knees shaking with relief. "Thanks for the ride."

He climbed back in the truck and drove off.

You were lucky this time, Spencer, I told myself, but you might not be so lucky again. I made up my mind that I would not hitchhike anymore, even if I had to crawl to Candlestick Park on my hands and knees. It was just too risky.

Instead, I climbed on the bike and started pedaling along the service road that ran parallel to the freeway. Toward evening I reached a town where I found a large park. Except for a man pushing a toddler on a swing, the park was deserted. I chose a picnic table away from the swings, near a grove of trees.

I ate the last apple and Aunt May's graham crackers for dinner. I intended to eat only half the crackers and save the rest for breakfast, but I was famished after riding my bike most of the day. I kept taking one more and one more, and before I knew it they were gone.

I ate the second Rice Krispies cookie, but I was still hungry. Even Foxey's cat food looked good to me. It looked good to Foxey, too, and he crunched down a lot of it.

While Foxey ate, I wrote a letter.

Dear Mama:
I am okay but I miss your cooking, especially the macaroni and cheese. Foxey is also okay. He misses the leftover macaroni.
Tell Aunt May she can quit praying for my soul because as soon as I get to Holly-

wood I will pay back the $14 I took out of
her purse. I will try to send some money for
you, too.

> *Your loving son,*
> *Spencer Atwood*

When I finished my letter, Foxey was washing his paws and whiskers. I watched the man take the toddler out of the swing, put him in a stroller, and walk away.

"Time for your walk," I told Foxey. I didn't see any molehills. We'd have to find a patch of dirt.

Foxey took his own sweet time about walking anywhere. First he had to look at the bottom of the picnic bench. Then he had to smell the wind, turning his head in every direction. Finally, after I nudged him in the rear with my toe, he slithered along the edge of the trees.

We had walked about five minutes when a boy my own size stepped out of the trees a few feet in front of us. Foxey and I stopped.

"Hey, Cat Man," the boy said. "What are you doing?"

"Taking a walk."

"You alone?"

I nodded.

"Me, too," he said.

There was a long pause while we looked at each

other. He wore jeans and a Mariners' sweatshirt. I wondered if he meant he was *really* alone, like I was, or if he was alone here at the park.

"Where do you live?" he asked.

"San Francisco."

"You planning to walk all that way with your cat?"

"I have a bike," I said.

There was more silence while he appeared to think that over.

"You got folks there?" he asked.

"My dad."

"I don't know where my dad is," he said. "Or my mom, either. I live with my sister."

"Around here?"

He pointed behind him. "Six blocks that way. I'm on my way to get dinner; this is the shortcut. You like spaghetti?"

"I love it. But I can't afford to eat at a restaurant."

"This place is cheap. If you carry the food out, you get a huge plate of spaghetti and two pieces of garlic toast for two dollars."

My mouth watered as I listened. "Is it plain spaghetti sauce or meat sauce?" I asked.

"Plain. Meatballs are an extra fifty cents each."

The boy dug into his pocket, pulled out three dollar bills, and showed them to me. "I'm getting two meatballs tonight," he said. He put the money away. "Usually, I only get the spaghetti."

It would be worth it, I decided. I needed a good meal, to keep my strength up, and I couldn't get that much food for two dollars at a grocery store.

"How far away is this place?" I asked.

"Four blocks. You want to come with me?"

I looked down at Foxey, who was tentatively scratching at a bare spot in the grass.

"I really need to walk my cat first. He's been shut in his box all day. Tell me how to get there; I'll go later."

"The restaurant closes at seven," he said, "and it's past six-thirty now. That's why the spaghetti is so cheap. The rest of the day, the same meal costs $4.95, but the owner starts fresh every morning, so the last half hour, he cuts the price."

I hesitated. I didn't want to make Foxey go back in the box before he had some exercise and a chance to go to the bathroom. On the other hand, a plate of spaghetti sounded great.

"I could get yours for you, if you want me to," the boy said. "I always bring mine back here and eat at a picnic table."

I thought it over. I didn't know anything about this kid. What if I handed over my two dollars and then he took off and I never saw him again?

"My name's Jay," he said.

I didn't want to tell him my name. "You can call me Cat Man," I said.

"I already did." Jay grinned. "What's your cat's name?"

"Foxey."

"He's beautiful."

That did it. Any kid who wore a Mariners' shirt and thought Foxey was beautiful couldn't be too rotten. I reached in my jeans pocket, took out my money, and handed Jay two one-dollar bills.

He took them. "Now!" he yelled.

An older boy, about sixteen, leaped out of the woods behind me. As I turned to look at him, he grabbed my wrist and tried to take the rest of the money out of my hand.

CHAPTER
SEVEN

I held tight to my money, and kicked at the older boy.

Foxey ran, pulling the rope taut. I clung to the end of the rope with my left hand while the bigger boy bent my right arm behind my back and attempted to pry my fingers open.

I twisted and jerked, trying to get away from him. He was bigger and stronger, but I was furious and my anger sent strength surging through my body.

"Help!" I yelled, turning toward Jay.

The word was barely out of my mouth, when Jay tackled me.

I landed face down on the grass. Jay jumped on me,

holding me down, while the other boy forced the money out of my hand.

"Got it!" the older boy said.

They both leaped up, and ran off through the trees.

Foxey was flopping with fear on the other end of the rope. I crawled across the grass to him, and crouched over him to help him feel safe. He leaned against me and stuck his head under my arm. He was trembling. So was I.

"It's okay," I told him. "They're gone. It's okay."

But it wasn't okay. It wasn't okay, at all. The boys had taken all of my paper money. The only money I had left was fifty-one cents in change.

How was I going to get to Candlestick Park with no money? What would I eat? How would I feed Foxey after he finished the one box of cat food?

I couldn't even report the boys to the police, even though I could give an accurate description of both of them. If I told the police what had happened, they'd want my name and start asking questions and pretty soon they'd figure out that I was a runaway kid and then they would make me go home.

Jay, if that was really his name, and his bully buddy were probably counting on that, I thought bitterly. That's why he asked me if I was alone, and where I was heading. They knew I wouldn't want to call the police. They knew if they stole my money, they'd get away with it.

There probably isn't an Italian restaurant, I thought. It was all a lie, to trick me into showing my money. And I was stupid enough to fall for it.

I sat quietly, stroking Foxey, until he relaxed and started to move around again. We finished his walk. I wasn't worried about the boys coming back; I knew they'd stay clear of me, now that they had what they wanted.

When it grew dark, I kicked some dead leaves into a pile, for my bed. I thought it would be softer than the ground. It was, a little, but every time I moved, the leaves crackled. Foxey didn't like that, and I didn't want to make any unnecessary noise, so I ended up on the ground again, just like the first night. My leg ached; I wished I had packed some aspirin.

I was exhausted, and fell asleep quickly despite listening for dog tags or voices. I awoke three times during the night: once with a cramp in my foot, and twice because Foxey was sleeping on top of my legs and I couldn't move. Each time, I lay wondering what to do next. I would have to abandon Plan A. Without money for food, I would never make it to Candlestick Park on a bike.

Splashes of pink colored the clouds the next time I awoke. I shifted a little without dumping Foxey off. He purred and dug his claws in and out of my jeans.

A new day and some sleep brought fresh determination. My injured leg felt better, too. Plan B, I decided, would be to call Dad and ask him to send me money for bus fare. Why hadn't I thought of that in the first place? For all I knew Dad had a great job with the Giants and made plenty of money. He might even send me enough for plane fare. Wouldn't that be something?

I walked Foxey around a little and then rode on, watching for a telephone booth. I wanted to make my call as soon as possible, before Dad left for work.

I spotted a phone booth near a gas station. I took my debt journal and pencil out of my backpack, so I could write down Dad's number. Then I stepped inside the phone booth, deposited my quarter, and pressed O.

"I want to make a collect call to San Francisco," I said, when the operator answered, "but I don't know the number."

"What's your party's name?" she asked.

"Atwood," I said, and spelled it for her. "His first name is Jerome."

"One moment, please."

I held the receiver with my left hand, and the pencil in my right hand.

"I'm sorry. There is no listing in San Francisco for a Jerome Atwood."

"Is there some other town that's close to Candlestick Park?" I asked.

"There are several," she replied. "Would you like me to check San Bruno?"

"Yes, please."

I was getting nervous. What if she couldn't find Dad's number?

"I'm sorry," the voice said again. "I don't find a listing for a Jerome Atwood anywhere in San Mateo County."

"Oh," I said. "Well, thanks anyway."

I hung up, hoping I would get my quarter back. It didn't come. I was down to twenty-six cents. I stood in the phone booth, looking out at the traffic whizzing past. Although the phone booth smelled as if someone had used it for a bathroom, I was not in a hurry to leave.

Who could I call that would help me? Other than Mama or Aunt May, that is. The only other phone number I knew by heart was Mike's, my friend from the school I went to before we moved.

Mike! As soon as I thought about him, I knew it was a good idea. Maybe Mike could loan me some money. He could send it in care of General Delivery at the next town on my map.

I got out the map and studied it. I figured it would take a day or two for Mike's letter to arrive. I decided to ask Mike to send as much money as he could to General Delivery in Salem, Oregon. Even if I didn't eat for two days, I would still be able to make it that far.

I deposited my last quarter, relieved when a different operator answered. I didn't want the telephone company getting suspicious.

This time I said, "I want to place a collect call." I gave Mike's number. I even knew the area code, since it was the same as mine used to be.

I heard the phone ring, and I heard Mike's mother say, "Hello?"

The operator said, "One moment, please," and then asked me, "What is your name?"

I thought fast. I couldn't give my real name. I was positive Mama would have called Mike's mother by now to say that I was missing. But if I made up a name, Mrs. Pinkus would not accept the charges. I realized I should have called person-to-person.

"I changed my mind, Operator," I said, and hung up. My quarter clanked into the coin return.

I tried one more time, this time specifying that the call was only for Mike Pinkus. Mike's mother answered again.

"I have a person-to-person call for Mike Pinkus," the operator said.

"Just a minute," Mrs. Pinkus said, and I could hear her call, "Mike! Telephone!"

"What is your name?" the operator asked me.

"Foxey," I replied.

Mike said, "Hello?"

The operator said, "I have a collect call from Foxey. Will you accept the charges?"

"No," said Mrs. Pinkus. "He most certainly will not."

My heart sank. Mike must have picked up an extension phone, and his mother had stayed on the line.

"But Mom," Mike said. "Foxey is . . ."

"Hang up, Michael," she said, "and tell your friends not to call here collect."

I hung up without saying anything else. Even though I had not talked to Mike, I was sure he had figured out who Foxey was. He knew I was trying to reach him.

I decided to try again about four o'clock. Maybe Mrs. Pinkus would not be there when Mike got home from school. Mike might try to stay home alone in case I called again. He would accept the next call without his mother knowing about it.

Meanwhile, I needed something to eat. I wished I had not been so greedy with the graham crackers the night before.

I mailed my letter to Mama before I pedaled south again. I wondered if she would believe I was really going to Hollywood.

EIGHT

An hour later, I stole a little kid's lunch box. A Batman lunch box.

It happened right after I stopped to let Foxey stretch. As I put him back in his box, I heard voices. Three little boys ran past me to the corner. They set their lunch boxes, backpacks, and coats on the curb, and began a game of tag in the yard of the corner house. They appeared to be about first-grade age, and they were obviously waiting for the school bus.

While I eyed the lunch boxes, the boys yelled and chased each other around.

Feeling like the number one rat of all time, I rode to the corner. When I reached the kids' pile of belongings, I stopped, bent down, and snatched the Batman lunch box. Then I pedaled away fast. The three kids didn't even notice.

First Aunt May's money, then the bike, and now a first-grader's lunch box. How low would I sink before I finally made it to Candlestick Park?

I paid attention to the cross streets as I sped off. After riding hard for a couple of miles, I found an empty lot, sat down under a tree, and looked to see what I was having for breakfast.

There was a peanut butter and grape jelly sandwich, with the crusts cut off, and a bag of corn chips. I should have swiped the Lion King lunch box. I had hoped for an orange or banana, and a can of juice, and maybe some cookies for dessert. I guess kids in first grade don't eat as much as I do. At least the sandwich wasn't chopped liver.

There was no identification on the lunch box.

After I ate, I took out my debt journal. I'll probably be forty years old before I can pay back all I owe.

I had no idea what the lunch box was worth, but five dollars seemed fair. I wrote:

3. Batman lunch box and lunch. $5.00
Owed to boy on corner of Maple and Fifteenth Street in . . .

I quit writing. He wouldn't get a letter addressed to a street corner. How could I mail five dollars to a kid if I don't know his name or his address?

I drew a line through what I had just written. On a fresh piece of paper I wrote, "Thank you for the lunch. I was very hungry." I put the note inside the lunch box, got on the bike, and rode back to the corner where I had taken the lunch box. The boys were gone.

I put the Batman lunch box on the curb, where the little boy would see it when he got off the bus. I hoped one of his pals would share his lunch with him today.

Still hungry, I rode on. I went through several small towns, and stopped three times to drink some water and to let Foxey out for exercise. I felt hungrier when I stopped than when I was pushing the pedals so I only rested a few minutes each time.

I saw a lighted sign on a bank that gave the time as 3:45. I decided to call Mike again. School got out at 3:20. With luck, Mike would answer the phone.

I found another phone booth and placed a person-to-person collect call. Mike answered.

"I have a call for Mike Pinkus," the operator said.

"This is Mike." His voice sounded odd, as if he didn't really want to talk to me.

"You have a collect call from Foxey," the operator said. "Will you accept the charges?"

"Yes. But tell him my mother . . ."

"Go ahead, please," said the operator.

"Hi, Mike. This is Spencer."

"Spencer Atwood, where are you?" said Mrs. Pinkus.

Spencer realized that Mike's mother had been on the line the whole time. That's why Mike sounded strained.

"Your mother is worried sick," Mrs. Pinkus said. "Tell me where you are and I'll come to get you."

I hung up. There was no point trying to call Mike. I would have to get some money another way.

I wasn't sure what town I was in. I rode along with my stomach growling. The peanut butter sandwich and corn chips had been seven hours ago. I had to get food, or money to buy it, soon.

A few blocks from the phone booth, I spotted a large grocery store. I left my bike at the end of a row of shopping carts in front of the building. I took Foxey, in his box, with me.

Two teenage girls sat at a card table just outside the store, selling candy bars. Every time someone approached, one of the girls said, "Would you like to buy a chocolate bar to support the high school band? We're raising money for new uniforms."

Most people replied, "How much?" and when the girls said, "One dollar," a lot of people handed over a dollar bill. One woman said, "I'll buy one, but you girls can eat it. I'm on a diet."

I wanted to say, "I'll eat it for you," but I knew that would seem weird and I probably looked weird enough already, carrying around a cardboard box with a cat in it.

I went into the store and asked the woman at the first check stand if I could talk to the manager.

"Upstairs," she said, pointing to a stairway at the other side of the store.

I climbed the steps and knocked on a closed door.

"Come in."

"Do you have any work I can do?" I asked.

He didn't answer right away. He just looked at me.

I swallowed hard, aware that my shirt was none too clean and it was three days since I'd had a shower.

"How old are you?" the manager asked.

"Thirteen." That was stretching it some, but thirteen sounds a lot older than twelve.

"I can't hire anyone younger than sixteen."

"You wouldn't have to pay me with money," I said. "You could just give me some food."

"Are you hungry, son?"

"Yes, sir."

"Where do you live?"

"I don't remember the address," I said. "I just moved." That wasn't really a lie, I decided.

"What do you have in that box?" he asked.

"Just something I don't want to lose. My daddy gave it to me." I hoped Foxey wouldn't choose that particular moment to test his vocal cords. I was pretty sure animals are not allowed in grocery stores.

He looked at me for a long moment. "Did you run away from home?" he asked.

"Oh, no, sir," I said. "I live with my Mama and my Aunt May but times are hard just now and I eat an awful lot. I thought if I earned some food before I go home, I wouldn't need so much dinner tonight."

The manager nodded at me. "Pick up all the litter in the parking lot," he said, "and put it in the trash bin behind the store." As he talked, he scribbled something on a slip of paper. "When you're finished, take this to the clerk in the deli section. He'll give you a sandwich and something to drink." He handed the paper to me.

"Thank you, sir," I said. "I'll do it right away."

I backed out of his office and closed the door behind me. I raced down the stairs, helped myself to a plastic bag from the end of a check stand, and went outside. There was plenty of trash blowing around the parking lot in front of the store.

I slid my left arm, which was holding Foxey's box, through the handles of the bag. I collected trash with the other hand and put it in the bag. I picked up losing lottery tickets, gum wrappers, an orange peel, empty soft-drink containers, store receipts, and a baby bottle that smelled like sour milk.

As I worked, I thought about the sandwich I was earning. If the deli had hot sandwiches, I would ask for grilled cheese. If they only had cold sandwiches, I'd get either cheese with lettuce and tomato, or egg salad. I wondered if the deli gave a dill pickle on the side. I hoped so. Maybe there would be little packets of mustard, too.

When the plastic bag was full, I carried it to the back of the store and emptied it into the trash bin. Then I went out to fill it again. Once I bent to pick up a Coke can and spotted a penny under a car. "I found a lucky penny," I told Foxey, as I put it in my pocket. "Now we have twenty-seven cents."

I felt even luckier when I saw a half-full bag of potato chips. I snatched it up, grabbed a handful, and stuffed them in my mouth, savoring the crisp, salty chips. As I chewed, the corner of my lip tickled.

I wiped my lip with my finger and glanced down at my finger. An ant crawled toward my wrist. A big black ant. I stopped chewing.

I flicked the ant to the pavement, opened the bag wide, and looked inside. The ant's relatives were having a party in my bag of potato chips. Dozens of them crawled around on the chips and on the inside of the bag. I spit the half-chewed contents of my mouth back into the bag, rolled the bag up tight, and hurried behind the store.

As I dropped the potato chips in the trash, I ran my tongue around the inside of my mouth, hoping I would find only my teeth.

I considered turning my piece of paper in to the deli clerk right then, since I desperately wanted to get the taste of those potato chips out of my mouth, but I had not yet finished picking up all the litter, and a deal's a deal. The store manager was nice enough to give me a job, and I did not intend to cheat him.

I headed out again. I was in the far corner of the parking lot, filling the bag for the third time, when the police car arrived. It cruised slowly, as if the occupants were looking over the whole area.

I dropped down behind a maroon minivan. Had the store manager called the police and told them he had found a suspected runaway? Had he asked me to pick up litter as a way to keep me here until the cops could come? I stood up just far enough to see what was happening, peeking over the top of the minivan.

The police car pulled into one of the handicap parking spaces closest to the store. One officer stayed in the car, with the motor running. A second officer got out and went inside. Through the glass window, I could see him talking to the manager.

My mouth went dry. They were looking for me; I was sure of it. Maybe the manager had seen my picture on the news, and he recognized me.

The police officer returned to the patrol car, and it cruised slowly up and down the parking lot. I stayed behind the minivan. As the police car turned down the row I was in, I dropped to my hands and knees and peered under the minivan. When I saw tires approaching, I crawled to the back end of the van and then around to the far side. The patrol car kept going.

When the officers had driven every row, the patrol

car double-parked in front of the store, and one cop went in again. A minute later, he came out. Then the patrol car drove out of the parking lot, and went off down the street. I crouched beside the minivan, watching.

I let out a huge sigh of relief as the patrol car disappeared from view.

"What are you doing?"

The voice was right behind me, so close that the hair on my arms stood on end as I turned to see who had spoken. It was a woman about Mama's age. She stood beside a cart load of groceries, with a car key in her hand.

"Why are you looking in my car?" she demanded. "Were you trying to break in?"

I realized this was the owner of the minivan.

"I'm playing hide-and-seek," I said. "I didn't bother your car any; I just used it to hide behind." I backed away from the van.

The woman carefully examined the side of her van, where I had been crouched, before she answered.

"A parking lot is not a safe place to play," she said. "What's wrong with parents these days, allowing their children to run wild?"

"Sorry," I said. I walked away from her toward my bike, keeping my eyes on the front window of the store, in case the manager was looking out.

I fingered the slip of paper in my pocket, longing to go to the deli counter and collect my sandwich. But

I knew I couldn't turn in the note. If I set foot in that store, the manager would be on the phone before the mustard for my sandwich hit the bread.

It wasn't fair not to get any pay after I did the work, but facts are facts. I had been lucky to spot the police before they spotted me. I couldn't take a chance that they would return.

With my stomach still grumbling, I tied Foxey's box on my bike, and took off. I pedaled the long way out of the parking lot, to avoid going past the front of the store. I also kept a sharp eye out for police cars.

I went six blocks and then stopped to think. I could wait until the night shift was on duty at the grocery store, and then go back and give my note to the deli clerk. But what if the store manager alerted the night crew? What if he told them to watch for me? By now, the whole store probably knew that if a kid came in with a note good for a sandwich and a drink, they were supposed to call the cops.

I rode on, looking for a bakery or a sandwich shop. Maybe I could buy day-old bread for twenty-seven cents. There was no point saving the quarter for a phone call, since I didn't have anyone to call. I might as well spend my fortune on food.

NINE

Two blocks ahead, golden arches curved against the sky. I knew I couldn't get anything for twenty-seven cents at McDonald's, but it was a good place to wash. The parking lot litter had left my hands sticky and dirty. I scrubbed good, rinsed out my mouth, and put on my clean T-shirt.

When I finished, I walked through the restaurant toward the door. As I passed a table where a woman, a man, and a little girl sat, the little girl said, "I'm not hungry."

"Eat your dinner," her mother said. "There are starving children in Bosnia who would give anything for those French fries."

Bosnia? I thought. There's a starving kid right here

beside you who would give anything for those French fries.

"I don't like French fries," the little girl said.

My mouth watered. On impulse, I sat down in the booth behind them, and listened. If the kid refused to eat her French fries, maybe they would get left on the table.

"I don't want the rest of my hamburger," the girl said.

"Oh, for heaven's sake," her father said. "I don't know why we bring her here. She doesn't eat enough to keep an ant alive."

I remembered the potato chips, and wished he hadn't mentioned ants.

"Can I go play now?" the child asked.

"One more bite," her mother said.

The girl took a tiny bite of the hamburger and then ran outside to the play area. Her mother stood up, gathering coats. Her father started to put the food containers on a tray.

I jumped to my feet. "I'll clear the table for you, sir," I said.

He looked surprised, but handed me the tray. "When did McDonald's start offering this service?" he asked his wife, as they headed toward the play area.

I put all of their things on the tray and carried them to a booth on the other side of the restaurant. I sat with my back to the play area, so they wouldn't recognize me if they happened to look my way.

I ate the French fries first, drenching them with catsup and savoring every bite.

I stared at the half-eaten hamburger, and debated what to do.

The problem was, I decided awhile back to be a vegetarian. Aunt May said I was out of my noggin. Mama said, "Don't be difficult, Spencer. It's hard enough to get a meal on the table without worrying about some cultish religious beliefs."

"It doesn't have anything to do with religion," I told her. "I just don't want to eat animals anymore. I like them too much. It's like eating a friend."

"Pigs are your friends now?" Mama said. "Chickens are your friends?"

"They have faces," I said.

"We don't eat the faces," Mama said. "Those animals are raised to become meat. That's their purpose."

"That doesn't make it right," I said. "Animals feel pain and fear, just like we do."

"That boy," said Aunt May, "is going 'round the bend."

"Suit yourself," Mama said, "but don't expect me to cook tofu casserole."

"He reads too much," Aunt May said. "That's the problem. He gets crazy ideas from books, and he thinks about them. Why can't he just watch cartoons, like my kids do?"

That first night, after I told Mama my decision, she fixed fried chicken. I took an extra helping of mashed potatoes and green beans, and ignored the platter of chicken.

I had expected it to be hard at first, to pass up meat. I thought I would feel deprived. Instead, I felt peaceful. That's the only word for it. Peaceful. I had wanted to be a vegetarian for a long time, and all that while I felt guilty every time I bit into a hamburger or swallowed a spoonful of turkey soup.

The plate of mashed potatoes and green beans was the first meal I'd eaten in months without imagining the eyes of the animal that gave its life for what I ate.

And so, with my empty stomach grumbling, I sat in McDonald's and stared at that little girl's hamburger. I knew if I did not eat it, it was going in the garbage can. It was too late to save the cow's life, but what about my life? If I was going to survive, I needed to eat.

I decided it's easier to have high moral standards when your stomach is full. I picked up the hamburger and took a bite.

I held it in my mouth for a moment without chewing, and then spit it into a napkin. I couldn't eat it. Not anymore.

I could almost hear Aunt May saying, "That boy is daft, for sure." Sometimes I suspected she was right.

I picked the remaining hamburger meat out of the bun, and ate the bun. I wrapped the meat in a paper napkin, and put it in my pocket. I couldn't save that cow's life, but I could save Foxey's, and I knew it wouldn't bother Foxey one bit to swallow that piece of meat.

I decided to stay at McDonald's for awhile, and offer to clear the tables for other people. There was probably a lot of wasted food in a place like this, and there was no reason why it shouldn't go in my stomach, instead of in the garbage can.

I wandered slowly from one end of McDonald's to the other, watching to see who was almost finished and what they might be leaving behind.

It took nearly an hour, but I managed to get most of a banana muffin, part of a chocolate milk shake, and two more half-full containers of French fries. I soon discovered that little kids were my best chance for leftovers, and I smiled whenever a family with small children placed an order.

Through all of this, I kept a close watch on my bike. Foxey's box was tied to it and I didn't want anyone bothering him.

It was past sunset before I left McDonald's and began to search for a place to spend the night.

For the first time since the boys had stolen my money, I felt optimistic. There had to be plenty of fast-food places between where I was and Candlestick Park. Maybe I could scrounge enough food each day to keep myself going.

I couldn't find another park to sleep in, so I settled for a schoolyard. I figured it would be quiet at night, and there was a soccer field where I could walk Foxey.

Foxey gobbled up the little girl's hamburger and then refused his cat food. I should have given him the cat food first, and saved the hamburger for dessert. I had refilled the water jar at McDonald's and he was glad to get a drink.

He seemed glad to explore the schoolyard, too. He trotted along, as if he knew where he was going, stopping once to sniff at the bottom of the slide.

It was almost dark by then, but a streetlight allowed me to see where we were going.

There was sand under the swings and Foxey decided it was the world's largest litter pan. When he finished, I used the napkin from the hamburger to pick up his deposit and throw it in the trash barrel. I didn't want some kid stepping in it the next day.

We bedded down against the back of the building. I had kept track of the days, and I knew the next day was Saturday. With any luck at all, no one would arrive at the school until I was wide awake and out of there.

For once, everything went as I had planned. I did not open my eyes again until daybreak. Foxey was already up, rooting around and trying to get in the backpack. He probably smelled his cat food.

With no hamburger to dull his appetite, he was plenty happy to eat the cat crunchies, and I gave him a long walk before I put him back in his box and started off.

I was more hungry than I had ever been in my life. I used to ask Mama for a snack before dinner and when she said *no*, I complained that I was starving to death. But I had never experienced true hunger before, and believe me, it isn't much fun. The leftover French fries seemed a lifetime ago.

I walked my bike through the business section of town, hoping for another fast-food restaurant where I could be the unofficial busboy. I didn't want to go back to McDonald's. I had ridden at least a couple of miles beyond that, and the last thing in the world I needed was to go backward.

When I reached the outskirts of town without spotting another restaurant, I went into a Quick Stop gas station/grocery store and looked around, hoping to find something I could afford. I saw nothing. There was a display of cookies on the checkout counter and I longingly eyed the individually wrapped chocolate chip cookies. They were huge—about four times the size of the ones Mama made. They were also seventy-nine cents each.

"May I help you?" asked the young man behind the counter.

"Do you sell anything for twenty-seven cents or less?" I asked.

He thought for a moment. "Just these," he said. He pointed to a fishbowl filled with chocolate-covered mint creams. "They're two for a quarter."

It would have to do. I took two mints and he rang

87

up the sale. Including sales tax, it came to twenty-seven cents. I handed it over and walked out.

I took tiny bites of mint and sucked each bite until it dissolved, making the candy last as long as possible, but my stomach did not even realize it was being fed. When the last piece of mint was gone, my belly hurt just as much as it had before I spent my money. My right leg felt okay, though. At least only one part of me hurts at a time.

All right, I told myself. There will be a McDonald's or a Burger King or something else in the next town.

It was time to put some miles on the bike. I rode hard all morning, stopping twice for water and to let Foxey out.

At the city of Longview, I crossed the Columbia River. The high, narrow bridge had no separate bike lane, so I had to ride on the shoulder. I pumped hard to get up the steep approach to the bridge and rode nervously across with cars whizzing by on my left and the long drop to the river on my right. By the time I reached the other side, I was dripping with sweat. But it was worth it; I was now in Oregon, and that seemed lots closer to my goal than Washington had.

It was past noon when I came to the town of Grafton. I walked my bike along the sidewalk on Main Street, looking down. Maybe I would get lucky and find some money. When I passed a pay telephone, I put my fingers in the coin return, just in case someone had forgotten to pick up their change. It was empty.

I passed an appliance store that had a row of television sets in the window. All of them were tuned to the same channel: a baseball game. I stopped to watch, and a tingle of excitement ran down the back of my neck.

"It's the Giants," I told Foxey. "The Giants and the Pittsburgh Pirates." My spirits rose and I stood close to the window, staring at one of the screens. It showed the score, and I saw that the Giants were batting in the bottom of the seventh. That means the Giants are home team, I thought. This game is being televised from Candlestick Park.

I took it as a good omen, and I watched carefully, hoping the camera would zoom in on the crowd. Maybe I would see Dad at the game! Wouldn't that be something?

That's where I'm going, I told myself. In another week, I'll be there, sitting in the stands with Dad, watching the Giants in person. We'll take along a big bag of peanuts in the shell, and later Dad will buy me a frozen malt or a soft drink.

"Are you a baseball fan?"

I jumped at the voice. An older man had joined me on the sidewalk. He held a bag of popcorn.

"Yes," I said. "Especially the Giants."

"Me, too. Used to play some ball myself, years ago. Never made it to the majors, but I had a great time anyway." He ate a handful of popcorn.

He wore a plaid shirt, and suspenders held his pants

up. His face looked like Santa Claus without a beard.

"Have some popcorn?" he asked, extending the bag toward me.

I heard Mama's voice in my mind: Never talk to strangers. Never accept food or money from someone you don't know.

I could smell the popcorn.

I stuck my hand in the bag. "Thanks," I said.

We watched the rest of the inning in silence. When the commercials came on, the man said, "Haven't seen you around before. You new in town, are you?"

"Just visiting," I said.

He offered the popcorn again, and this time I accepted immediately.

"You think the Giants have a chance at the World Series?" he asked.

"They're a cinch," I said.

He laughed. "I hope you're right."

We watched another half inning and then the man said, "I've had enough popcorn. Do you want the rest, or should I toss it?"

"I'll take it," I said. "Thanks."

He handed me the half-full bag, and I gobbled up all but the last inch, which I saved for Foxey. Right at that moment, popcorn tasted even better than Mama's macaroni and cheese.

The man watched me eat, but said nothing.

Pittsburgh went down one-two-three in the top of the ninth, which ended the game.

"Why did you save some of the popcorn?" the man asked, pointing at the sack, which I had carefully folded so the popcorn wouldn't spill.

"It's for my cat."

"Is your cat hungry?"

"Not right now. I have some cat food, but it might not last as long as it needs to, so I feed him other things when I can."

"My cat died not long ago," the man said, "and I still have a couple of boxes of cat food at home. If you want to come home with me, you can have them."

I hesitated. What if the old man was some sort of crazed child molester? What if he locks kids in his closets and lets them starve to death? I had been too gullible when I believed that Jay was going to buy me a plate of spaghetti. I couldn't afford another bad choice.

"You wouldn't have to come inside, if you don't want to," the man said. "I know your folks have probably told you never to go anywhere with a stranger."

I nodded.

"It's just a few blocks," he said, and started off down the sidewalk.

What if he's an ax murderer? I thought. What if I'm making another stupid mistake?

But free cat food doesn't come along every day of the week.

I followed the man home.

CHAPTER

TEN

He lived in a small, old house with a front porch. Three-story apartment buildings crowded close on both sides.

"You can wait on the porch, if you like," the man said. "I'll bring it out."

I sat on the steps while the man went inside. Soon he returned with a bag containing three boxes of cat food. One was half full; the other two had never been opened. In his other hand, he carried a small tray that held a huge slice of cheese pizza and a glass of apple juice.

"I thought maybe the cat wasn't the only hungry one," he said, as he set the tray on the step beside me.

"Thanks."

"My name is Hank Woodworth."

I took a bite of the pizza.

"When I was sixteen years old," Hank said, "I ran away from home. Thought I'd see the world, be independent."

I stopped chewing and looked at him.

"It wasn't as easy as I thought it would be. Ran out of money after only three days."

"What did you do?"

"I went back home. My parents were so glad to see me that they didn't even wallop me, but you know something?"

"What?"

"I regretted going back so soon. I always wondered what would have happened if I'd tried a little harder to make it on my own before I gave up. 'Course, I was older than you. It's easier to find work when you're sixteen."

I opened Foxey's box and poured some of the cat food into it.

"Wouldn't he eat better if you took him out of that box?"

"He gets nervous in a strange place."

"You could take him inside, in the kitchen. It would be quiet and he could prowl around a bit."

I hesitated. I knew Foxey would love to be off the leash for a little while but I'd learned the hard way not to be too trusting.

"Look," Hank said. "I admire your caution. Shows

you aren't a fool who believes everything he's told. But there's a time to have faith, too, and this is one of those times."

I remembered an old movie I'd seen, where the sheriff said, "Look 'em in the eye. You can tell if a man's shifty or honest if you look 'em straight in the eye."

I looked into Hank Woodworth's eyes. They were a deep gray-blue and there were lots of crinkly lines at the edges, as if he smiled a lot. He was not my idea of an ax murderer.

"Foxey would like to eat in the kitchen," I said, and followed Hank Woodworth into the house.

Later, after Foxey had polished off a good bit of cat food and I had finished a second piece of pizza, I told Hank Woodworth the truth, the whole truth, and nothing but the truth. Who I am, where I was going, and why.

Hank listened quietly, nodding occasionally. Not once did he tell me I should not have lied to my mother. Not once did he warn me about the dangers of traveling alone. Not once did he suggest that I was a stupid, headstrong kid who didn't know what was good for him. There aren't many adults like Hank, I can tell you. All he said was, "Why don't you rest here overnight? I have some chores that need doing, so you'll be expected to earn your keep."

I mowed the lawn, weeded the front flower bed, and swept the sidewalk. Foxey jumped on and off the kitchen chairs, chased his tail, and rolled in a patch of sunlight on the linoleum. It felt good to both of us to move around without looking over our shoulders all the time.

While I worked and Foxey played, Hank cooked. When I went inside to tell him I'd finished all the chores, the house smelled like Mama's spaghetti. I sniffed appreciatively.

"You like polenta?" Hank asked.

"I've never had it," I said and then quickly added, "but it smells good."

"It's like spaghetti and meat balls, except there's cornmeal instead of meat."

"Sounds great. I don't eat meat, anyway."

"Neither do I," he said. We grinned at each other.

"Is there anything else you want me to do?" I asked.

"Yes."

I waited.

"After we eat, I want you to call your mother."

I shook my head.

"She must be worried about you. It isn't right not to let her know you're okay."

"I sent her a letter."

"That isn't the same as hearing your voice. You could have been forced to write a letter."

"If I call, she'll come after me. She'll make me go home."

"You don't need to tell her where you are. Just tell her you're all right."

"What if she has the call traced?"

"We'll call from a pay phone."

I shook my head again. "Mama could still find out the town."

"I'll pay for the call, so there won't be an operator involved."

I hesitated. Even if Mama traced the call to Grafton, it would take awhile for her to get here, and she wouldn't know where to find me once she arrived. And I was leaving in the morning.

"It's homemade spaghetti sauce," Hank said.

The polenta was delicious. Foxey thought so, too.

After we ate and did the dishes, I walked beside Hank to the pay phone downtown.

While he dropped quarters in the slot, he said, "You only get three minutes, so talk fast."

Aunt May answered the phone. When I said, "Hello, Aunt May," she screamed. I'll probably be deaf in my right ear for the rest of my life, the way she shrieked into the receiver. Then, without so much as a hello or how are you, she yelled, "Leona! It's him!"

I held the receiver away from my head in case Aunt May decided to shriek something else but instead she said, "Where are you?"

"Hollywood," I lied.

"No, you aren't," Aunt May said. "There's no way you could get all the way to Hollywood so soon unless you sprouted angel wings and I highly doubt a sneaky boy who steals money from his aunt, and disappears

96

for days on end, and scares his poor mama out of her wits, is about to sprout any angel wings."

Mama came on the phone then. "Spencer? Spencer, is it really you?"

"It's me, Mama," I said. "I called to tell you everything is fine."

"Everything is NOT fine," Mama said. "How can everything be fine when I don't know if my only child is alive or not? For all I know, you're lying dead in a gutter somewhere."

"I'm not in a gutter," I said. "If I was dead, I would not be able to dial a telephone."

"Where are you?"

"Hollywood."

"Already? How did you get there so soon?"

"I hitchhiked."

"Hitchhiked!" Mama's voice was nearly as shrill as Aunt May's had been. I winced and held the phone farther from my ear. "You know better than to hitchhike. You take your life in your hands when you hitch a ride. Anyone could pick you up. Anyone! You don't know who's behind the wheel of a car these days. It could be an ax murderer. The minute you get in that car, he could pull out his ax and split your skull in two. The last thing you'll see on this Earth is your own brains spilling out across some stranger's steering wheel."

"Nobody split my skull, Mama. I'm okay and Foxey's okay, too."

"You still have that fool cat with you?"

That question surprised me. Of course I still had Foxey. Why did she think I left?

"I thought he would run off before you got six blocks from home," Mama said.

"Well, he didn't."

Hank tapped his wristwatch and I knew the three minutes were nearly over.

"I have to go now, Mama," I said.

"Go?" she cried. "Go where?"

"Back to my friend's house."

"What friend? Who are you staying with?"

"Good-bye, Mama."

"Wait!" Mama said. "I'll pay for the call. I have to write down your number so I can . . ."

An operator interrupted. "If you wish to continue your call, please deposit another two dol-"

I hung up. I didn't want Mama to hear how much the call had cost because if she did, she might call the phone company and they could figure out how far away I was and I wasn't nearly far enough away to want her to know the distance.

I stood with my hand on the telephone receiver and a quivery feeling in the pit of my stomach. It had seemed strange to hear Mama's voice. I had pretty much convinced myself that if I never saw Mama again, it would be just fine with me, after the way she treated Foxey. But somehow, standing there by the drugstore, with the cars driving by and a faint breeze blowing, I was sorry the call didn't last longer. It was good to hear Mama's voice again, even though she was mad at me for running away.

"Want to call back?" Hank's voice snapped me out of my homesickness.

"No."

"Nothing wrong with changing your mind," he said. "Maybe running off was the right thing to do last week. Maybe going back is the right thing to do this week."

"I can't take Foxey back to Aunt May's."

"I could probably find a good home for Foxey."

"Foxey *has* a good home. With me."

Hank started to say something, changed his mind, and instead went in the drugstore and ordered two chocolate ice-cream cones for us to eat on the way home.

"How come you're being so nice to me?" I asked.

"I'm lonely. I miss having someone around to talk to. And you remind me of myself, when I was your age. You're a thinker, like I was."

When we got back to Hank's house, he cut a small hole in the bottom end of a brown paper bag and put the bag on the floor. Foxey instantly went inside the bag to investigate. Then Hank tapped the outside of the bag with a pencil, right next to the small hole. Foxey's paw shot out through the hole, feeling for the pencil. Hank tapped the other end of the bag, and Foxey did a quick *U*-turn.

Hank handed the pencil to me. "No sense spending money on expensive cat toys," he said. "All cats love a paper bag with a hole in the bottom."

Hank sat at his table, whittling a piece of wood. I sat on the floor, playing with Foxey. When Foxey tired of the bag-and-pencil game, Hank gave me a piece of string. I trailed it across the floor, and Foxey chased it.

"I worked all my life as a cabinetmaker," Hank told me. "Always did like to make things out of wood. Had to retire a few years back because of a heart attack, but I still whittle a couple of hours every day."

"Did you make those?" I asked, pointing to the carved wooden cats in various poses that lined Hank's windowsill.

"Yes."

"Did you copy your own cat?" I asked.

"Yep. He was a good cat. My wife named him Butter, because of his color." Hank sighed. "Those were good days," he said, "when Lois and Butter were still with me. But I can't go back to the past."

I knew exactly what he meant. There were good days in my past, too; days of story heroes named Spencer, and Saturday afternoon baseball games. But I couldn't go back anymore than Hank could.

CHAPTER
ELEVEN

I took a hot shower and went to bed early. It felt wonderful to sleep on a mattress, with a pillow under my head. I didn't hear a thing until eight o'clock the next morning.

I found Hank in the kitchen frying hash-brown potatoes while Foxey rolled around biting his piece of string.

"You want to stick around a couple of days?" Hank asked. "Learn how to whittle?"

I was tempted. I could picture Foxey and me settling in with Hank, but I knew if I wanted to get to Candlestick Park before the baseball season ended, I couldn't dawdle about.

After breakfast, Hank fixed some sandwiches for my

backpack. I laid them carefully on top of the boxes of cat food. Foxey was not at all happy about getting in his box but I told him there are some things in life you have to do whether you like it or not.

Hank watched as Foxey growled and struggled to get out of the box. "Last night, you said Foxey has a good home. I'm not so sure Foxey would agree."

I looked at Hank. Foxey took advantage of my inattention and leaped out of the box. He ran behind Hank's sofa.

"Cats aren't meant for traveling around, meeting new situations day after day," Hank said. "I'd bet anything that Foxey is scared half out of his fur every time he hears a dog bark, or a truck rattle past."

I bit my lip and looked away, knowing Hank spoke the truth.

"Sometimes," Hank said, "if you really love someone, you have to do what's best for them, even if it isn't what you want."

"If I take Foxey back to Aunt May's, I won't be able to keep him," I said. "I'd rather have him be scared while we travel than to go home and turn him in to the pound. He'd be terrified there, and if he didn't get adopted in a few days, he'd be killed."

"I'm not suggesting that you give him up. You can leave him here with me while you go on to Candlestick Park and find your dad. When you're all settled and have a good place for Foxey, you can let me know and we'll arrange to get him to you."

I knew Hank was right. Foxey would be much happier here, rolling on Hank's kitchen floor and sleeping where it's warm and dry, than he would be shut in a box all day, sleeping where it's cold and damp, and getting chased by strange dogs.

But it was scary to think of going on without Foxey. Even though he couldn't possibly protect me from any danger, it was comforting to have him with me.

"The whole reason I left home was so Foxey and I could stay together," I said. "I know you'd be good to him, but . . ."

My voice trailed away, and I swallowed hard. I couldn't leave Foxey behind. Without Foxey, I would be all alone.

I felt Hank's hand on my shoulder. "He'll probably get used to being on the road," Hank said, "especially if you keep feeding him Big Macs."

I fished Foxey out from under the sofa and this time he accepted his fate. He went limp as I put him in the box.

Hank wrote his address and phone number on a slip of paper. "If you need help," he said, "call me collect, any time—day or night. Or come back here, if you need a place to bunk."

"Thanks," I said. "Thanks for everything."

"Promise me you'll call if you need help."

"I promise."

"Safe journey," he said.

Hank held out his hand and I shook it. When I took

my hand away, there were two twenty dollar bills in my palm.

"The Greyhound Bus office is in a health food store, just down the street from the appliance store where we watched the ball game," he said. "The bus stops right in front, and it leaves for San Francisco at noon."

I threw my arms around Hank and hugged him.

"I wish I had more to give you," he said, "but it's the end of the month. Money's always tight then and I don't like to dip into my savings unless it's an emergency."

"I'll repay you," I said, "as soon as I can."

"This isn't a loan; it's a gift."

He went out on the porch and watched me leave. At the corner, I looked back and waved, thinking how odd it was that a man old enough to be my grandfather had become my best friend.

BUS TICKETS. The sign was inside the health food store, just as Hank had said. I walked to the counter.

"I'd like a ticket to San Francisco," I said.

"One way or round trip?"

"One way. Can my bike go in with the luggage?"

"It can if it's a collapsible bike. You can't take your cat, though." She pointed toward the front window.

I turned and looked. Foxey's head stuck out between the lid and the bottom of the box, and he was trying to squeeze out. The rubber bands that secured the top of the box to the bottom broke, and Foxey jumped to the ground.

I dashed for the door, but as soon as I was outside, I stopped. I knew if I moved too fast, Foxey might panic and run.

"Hey, big guy," I said softly. "You don't want to run loose around here. This is no place for a cat." While I talked, I inched toward him.

Foxey crouched beside the bike, with his tail flapping nervously from one side to the other. His big eyes stared at me.

I kept talking, hoping to keep him calm. "I know you don't like being cooped up in the box," I said, "and I'm sorry you have to do it. But it's better than being a cat pancake in the middle of the street, which is what will happen if you run away from me."

I was only a couple of feet away, getting set to grab him, when a car pulled up to the curb directly in front of us. Foxey bolted into the alley that ran along one side of the building.

I dashed after him, and saw him go under a large trash container that was on big wheels. I knelt on the pavement and peered under the trash container. The smell of rotting garbage surrounded me.

Foxey huddled against the wall of the building. I reached under and grabbed his front leg. When I tried to pull him out, he resisted, but I dragged him out, anyway. When his head emerged, he hissed at me.

Foxey had never hissed at me before. I held him close and, in my mind, I replayed my earlier conversation with Hank.

Hank was right, I admitted. Foxey doesn't have a good home with me, not anymore. If Foxey had a good home he would not be cowering under a garbage container in an alley, shaking with fear.

I sat on the pavement, with the garbage smell making me sick to my stomach, and felt tears trickle down my cheeks. Foxey stayed on my lap, with his face buried in my jeans. He quit trembling, but he didn't purr.

"I love you, Foxey," I whispered. "I love you too much to make you go any farther with me."

After a few minutes, I wiped my face on the bottom of my T-shirt and stood up. I stuffed Foxey back into his box and put the lid on it. I held the box shut while I walked the bike back to Hank's house.

Hank's face lit up when he opened the door and saw me.

"I can't take the bike along," I said. "Will you keep it here for me?"

"You can put it in the shed, out back," Hank said.

When I didn't move toward the shed, he added, "The one where I keep the lawn mower."

"Greyhound buses don't allow animals, either," I said. "I'd like you to keep Foxey until I find my dad." I handed him the box.

Hank carried it inside, put it on the floor, and removed the lid. Foxey looked around. When he saw where he was, he stepped out, stretched his hind legs, and sauntered toward the kitchen. He never looked back to see if I was coming, too.

I took the boxes of cat food out of my backpack and gave them to Hank.

"I'll take good care of him," Hank said. "In fact, I'll probably spoil him rotten."

I nodded, not trusting myself to talk about Foxey.

"Call me anytime, and I'll tell you how he's doing."

I nodded again. Then I hurried out the door and walked away. Alone.

I sensed that Hank watched me until I got to the corner, but I didn't turn to wave. *It's only temporary*, I told myself. *I'll be back soon to get Foxey and then I'll never leave him again. Never.*

The bus was pulling in when I got there. Quickly, I bought my ticket.

"The bus leaves in ten minutes," the ticket clerk said.

"Could I use your phone?" I asked. "It's a local call."

She nodded and set the telephone where I could reach it. I took the piece of paper with Hank's number on it out of my pocket, and dialed.

I wanted to ask Hank about Foxey. I wanted to know where he was at that very second, and what he was doing.

But when Hank answered, the words stuck in my throat, and I was afraid if I spoke, I would start to cry again.

"Hello?" Hank said. "Hello?"

I replaced the receiver, and climbed aboard the bus.

I found a window seat, but I didn't look out. I felt utterly alone without Foxey. I kept my backpack on my lap instead of storing it under my seat; I needed something to hold onto.

After awhile, I took out my debt journal and recorded everything Hank had paid for: the long-distance phone call to Mama, food, and the forty dollars. Even though he had told me not to repay him, I wanted to do it. I didn't want Hank going without in order to help me.

The bus ride to San Francisco took sixteen hours. The bus stopped in several towns and I got off twice to stretch and use the bathroom. Many passengers bought meals at these stops; I ate the sandwiches that Hank had packed for me.

At one stop, a young man boarded the bus and took the seat beside me. As soon as he was seated, he took a package of gum out of his pocket and unwrapped one stick. Then he offered the pack to me.

"Thanks," I said, as I took a stick of gum.

"Where are you headed?" he asked.

"Candlestick Park." As soon as I said it, I wished I hadn't. I had told Hank the truth, but I didn't want anyone else to know my destination. What if this man saw my face on a milk carton or a MISSING poster? He would tell Mama exactly where to find me.

"It isn't called Candlestick Park anymore," he said. "They renamed it. It's 3COM Park."

"Why?" I said. "What does that mean?"

"3COM is a big computer company. They paid to have the ballpark named after them."

"But Candlestick Park is a tradition," I said. "It's where Mays and McCovey played. The San Francisco Giants have always played in Candlestick Park."

"I heard the city got big bucks for changing the name."

I didn't want to believe him, but I knew the arena in Seattle, where the Sonics play basketball, was named Key Arena because Key Bank paid a lot of the construction cost.

I closed my eyes and thought about it. Dad's big dream had been to play baseball in Candlestick Park. And my dream was to live nearby and watch the Giants' games there, with him. I knew the ballpark was the same, but somehow our dreams seemed a bit tarnished if it wasn't Candlestick Park anymore. I decided the city of San Francisco could call the ballpark whatever they chose, but *I* would still call it Candlestick Park.

With that decided, I fell asleep. I woke up at every stop, but stayed on the bus and quickly dozed off again when we started moving. The next time I got off, I was in San Francisco. It was four A.M. as I walked into the bus terminal.

Now what? I thought. Several times during the bus ride, I had pictured myself walking into Candlestick Park. Somehow, I had never figured out how I was going to get there from the bus terminal, or what I would do until it was time for the ball game. I wished I had the bike with me.

The other passengers who got off went past the small waiting area, and down an escalator. I followed.

The old building was called the Transbay Transit Terminal; it was built on a hill. After taking a second down escalator, I reached street level. I went outside, to look around.

As I walked away from the building, a trio of young men with shaved heads and nose rings swaggered toward me. They wore studded dog collars around their necks; heavy chains dripped from their waists. I gave them plenty of room on the sidewalk, but they moved over, and blocked my way.

"Hey, kid," one of them said. "What's in the backpack?"

I turned and ran back into the bus terminal, hoping the chain gang would not pursue me.

CHAPTER

TWELVE

I rode up the escalators; the three men didn't follow. I passed the TV monitors that showed Greyhound arrival and departure times, and settled
into an uncomfortable black metal chair. I would stay
in the terminal until daylight.

I ate my last sandwich and bought a root beer from
a vending machine, feeling as lonely as if I were on a
deserted island. After I ate, I closed my eyes and
thought about my bed at home. Not Aunt May's
couch, my old bed in the house we used to rent.

When I was little, I never wanted to go to bed. I
tried every trick I could think of to get Mama to let
me stay up longer and then, when she finally insisted,
it always felt so good to slip between the sheets and

pull the striped blanket up under my chin, and close my eyes.

Mama used to come in my room, to "tuck me in." That meant she straightened the blanket, and kissed me goodnight.

After I got to be about ten, she didn't kiss me goodnight anymore, but she still came in. She stood beside my bed for a moment and then said, "Goodnight. Sleep tight."

By then I had Foxey, and most nights Foxey would jump up beside me and purr while I rubbed his head.

A lump rose in my throat when I thought about Foxey. When I left Foxey with Hank, I knew I would miss him, but I didn't know I would miss him so much. I felt as if a part of myself—a hand or a foot—was missing. I wondered what Foxey was doing.

I wondered what Mama was doing, too. I tried to picture her, at Aunt May's house. Was she asleep in the bottom bunk bed in Cissy's room? Was she sitting at the kitchen table drinking iced tea and worrying that I was lying dead in a gutter? Did she even care anymore? Maybe by now she was so disgusted at me for running away that she had disowned me, the way she was always threatening to do. Maybe I wasn't her kid anymore.

I pushed the thought away, and tried to concentrate on good things. I had made it to San Francisco. Foxey was safe, and I had not been chopped to pieces by an ax murderer. I should be happy. I should be ecstatic!

So why did I slump in the chair and feel like crying?

Because I was tired, and alone, and scared, that's why. I had some humongous problems which I had just thought of, and I spent the next hour worrying about them.

Problem number one: what if the Giants were not playing at home today? What if they were in Chicago or New York or Montreal? Just because they played at Candlestick the day Hank and I watched the game in the appliance store window did not mean they would be playing there today.

It could be a week or more before they had another home game, and where would I stay while I waited? Too late, I realized I should have found out the Giants' schedule while I was still at Hank's house. If the team was on the road, I could have stayed with Hank until they came home.

Problem number two, which I did not think of until after I bought the root beer: even if the Giants were scheduled to play at Candlestick today, how was I going to get in? The five dollars I had left might not be enough for a ticket.

The minutes crawled by while I worried. Some time after five o'clock, I finally dozed off in my chair.

I awoke shortly before seven when a family with four children noisily took seats beside me. While the kids squabbled over who would sit by the window after they got on the bus, their parents calmly read *The San Francisco Chronicle*.

When the next bus pulled in, the man laid the newspaper on an empty chair, picked up a suitcase, and helped his wife herd the children through the glass door to where the buses load. I snatched the newspaper, scanned the sports section, and blew out my breath in relief. The Giants were playing at home. Starting time: 1:05.

I needed to be there at least two hours early because Dad always liked to watch batting practice. I would stand at the main gate and wait for him to arrive.

The man at the Greyhound ticket counter told me I could find city bus information on the second floor. A whole wall was covered with maps and bus schedules. It took awhile, but I found what I needed: the 9X bus to the ballpark. The round-trip price for age twelve and under was three dollars. My arms prickled with excitement as I wrote down how to get to that bus stop. The bus ran every fifteen minutes, starting at 9:15.

At 8:30 I left the bus terminal, looking both ways in case more weirdos in chains were lurking nearby. Seeing none, I hurried to the corner of Market and Sutter. I was far from alone as I waited. Tall buildings reached high into the morning fog; cars, buses, and people bustled past.

An orange and white bus pulled up; the sign over the driver's window said BALLPARK EXPRESS. I asked if I could buy a one-way ticket, but the driver said no, so I handed over three dollars.

Half an hour later I saw the ballpark, and the water of San Francisco Bay, from the bus window. A big sign said 3COM Park. Right then, I didn't care what they called it.

The bus stopped in front of Gate B. I went to the ticket window and asked how much the cheapest seat cost.

"How old are you?" the ticket seller asked.

"Twelve." I hoped that meant I qualified for a kids' price.

"Pavilion seats for children are $3.50," the ticket seller said, "but fans fourteen and under must be accompanied by an adult."

"Oh." I stepped away. Even if I had enough money, which I didn't, I wouldn't be able to get in by myself.

The ballpark, like the Transit Terminal, was built on the side of a hill. Below me, toward the water, I saw the main parking lot. People who parked there entered through a different gate.

Unsure where to wait for Dad, I walked to the lower level. The open tailgate of one station wagon held a bowl of potato salad, slices of watermelon, and a loaf of sourdough bread. People sat in lawn chairs circling a barbecue; steaks sizzled on the grill.

Excitement crowded the hunger pangs out of my stomach as I passed the tailgate picnic. I was here. I was standing outside Candlestick Park, just as I had dreamed of doing. A feeling of exultation made the back of my scalp prickle. I had made it!

115

For a few minutes, I watched fans leave their parked cars, and head toward the escalators that carried them into the stadium, but my instincts told me that Dad would come by bus. When he still lived with me and Mama, he always took the bus to work. I walked back up to Gate B, where the buses arrive, and waited.

Buses disgorged people wearing Giants' caps and shirts. My eyes scanned back and forth. I had to spot Dad before he went in.

A young man stopped about six feet from me and held three tickets in the air. Soon two women asked him, "How much?"

"Ten bucks each," he said. "They're thirteen-dollar box seats but my friends couldn't make it."

One of the women handed him a twenty-dollar bill. "We'll take two," she said.

The young man noticed me watching. "Hey, kid," he said. "You want to buy a ticket, cheap?"

"I only have two dollars," I said.

He continued to hold the single ticket out, but nobody else stopped.

As one o'clock neared, the approaching crowd thinned, and so did my optimism. What if I had missed Dad? What if he had gone in a different gate?

When I heard "The Star-Spangled Banner," I bit my lip to keep the tears back, knowing it was almost game time.

All of my energy had focused on getting to Candlestick Park, and finding Dad. What if he hadn't come today? That postcard was three months old. Maybe he no longer . . . No. I refused to think that. If I had missed him going in, I would wait until the game was over and try to find him as he left. And if I didn't find him today, I'd come back tomorrow and stand outside a different gate.

The young man with the extra ticket said, "Are you okay, kid?"

I blinked fast and nodded. "I was supposed to meet my dad, but I think I missed him. He must have gone in."

The man handed me the ticket he had been trying to sell. "Here," he said. "You can have it. It will go to waste otherwise."

"Thanks," I said. "Thanks a lot!" Then, remembering the fourteen-and-under rule, I added, "Could I go in with you?"

"Sure."

We entered together and the ticket taker didn't give me a second glance.

"Play ball!" The call resounded through the park as we walked in. The man who gave me the ticket headed for a refreshment stand; I headed straight into the seating area. I didn't bother to look at the aisle number on my ticket because I didn't intend to sit in the seat, anyway. I wasn't there to watch baseball; I was there to find Dad.

I started down the aisle, looking at the people to my right. Halfway down an usher stopped me. "May I see your ticket, please?" he asked.

I held out my ticket.

"You're in the wrong section," he said. "You want Section Ten, not Section One."

"Sorry," I said, as I turned and climbed back up the steps.

I saw ushers posted partway down most aisles. How could I search the seats if I couldn't get close to them?

At the top of the next section, I followed a group of six people down the steps, and the usher assumed I was with them. When they sat down, I continued down the aisle to the end and then walked slowly back up again, scanning the faces on both sides.

I continued around the stadium, stopping at the entrance to each section. A few times, there was no usher and I walked slowly, looking carefully at the people on both sides of the aisle. At other sections, I stood in back and let my eyes rove back and forth, searching for the one face in all the world that I needed to find.

I had gone through half the lower level when it occurred to me that Dad would probably buy a less expensive seat, especially if he came every day. I walked up to the second level, where I knew seats would be cheaper. By the bottom of the fourth inning, I had strolled through every upper-level section where anyone was sitting.

It would be easy to miss him, I told myself. Maybe

he was in the bathroom when I passed his seat, or out buying a hot dog. Just because I didn't see him the first time around, doesn't mean he isn't here. Or maybe he *does* sit in the lower level.

I went back to the lower box seats and started where I had left off. The ushers didn't seem to be checking tickets anymore. Maybe by that time in the game, they didn't care whether people were in the right seat or not.

I was near the Phillies' dugout when I heard his voice. "To your right," he said. "Second aisle down."

I whirled around. He wore gray slacks, and a jacket that was black on the bottom, and half orange and half white on top. A photo ID hung around his neck and his black and orange baseball cap said "Guest Services." Dad was an usher!

I stood only six feet away, and saw him direct an elderly couple to their seats. Then he turned to watch the game.

My throat felt tight. Although I wanted to rush over and fling my arms around him, I was suddenly shy. Dad was shorter than I remembered—or was I just taller? He was thinner, too. But the face was the same and I realized with a jolt how much I resemble him.

He must have sensed someone staring at him, because he looked away from the field, directly at me. Surprise flashed across his face. "Spencer?" he said.

My shyness evaporated. I ran to him, and hugged him hard.

He laughed, stepped back, and looked me over from head to toe. "I almost didn't know you," he said. "You're nearly as tall as I am." He looked over my shoulder, as if expecting someone else. "What are you doing here?" he asked. "Where's your mother?"

"She isn't with me. She's still in Seattle."

We moved to the top of the aisle, where we wouldn't block anyone's view.

"Who brought you here?"

"Nobody. I came alone, to find you."

"What? You ran away?"

"Mama didn't have the rent money, and we had to move in with Aunt May, and Mama said I couldn't keep Foxey."

"Foxey? You still have that orange cat?"

"Mama said Foxey had to go to the pound, so I took him and left." I talked faster and faster. "I knew I'd find you here," I said. "I knew if I could just make it to Candlestick Park, you'd let me and Foxey live with you."

"You came alone? All the way from Seattle?"

I nodded.

"How did you get here?"

"I rode a bike part of the way, and then a man gave me money for bus fare."

"Whoa," Dad said, and rubbed his chin. "Does your mother know where you are?"

"No. But she knows I'm okay. I sent her a letter, and I called her once."

He shook his head. "Leona must be having fits," he said. "She probably thinks you're lying in the gutter, hacked to death by an ax murderer."

I laughed. It felt good to laugh again.

"How did you know where to find me?" Dad asked.

"You sent a postcard of Candlestick Park. Remember? So I knew you'd be here. And I knew you'd let me keep Foxey, because you let me have him in the first place."

"Where's the cat now?" Dad asked.

"My friend, Hank—the man who gave me bus money—is keeping Foxey until we send for him."

Just then a foul ball dropped into the seats ahead of us. Three fans scrambled to catch it, falling over each other as if the ball were solid gold. Dad hurried forward to make sure that nobody had been hurt in the scuffle.

When he returned, he said, "You took me by surprise, you know."

"I tried to call you; there wasn't any number listed. And I didn't have an address, so I couldn't send you a letter."

"Well, look," Dad said. "I need to keep working. You sit down and watch the rest of the game."

"Great," I said. I got out my ticket and looked to see where my seat was.

"There are empty seats in this section today," Dad said. "Sit right there." He pointed to a seat not far from where we stood.

I sat down, but I couldn't concentrate on the game. I was too happy, and too relieved. I felt as if I had just hit a tie-breaking grand slam. I wanted to clench my fists and shake them over my head, or give high fives to everyone around me. When it was time for the seventh-inning stretch, I sang, "Take Me Out to the Ball Game" as loudly as I could.

I watched as Dad helped people who were lost, and again when another foul ball came into our section.

Pride surged through me as I looked at him. Dad was living his dream; he spent every day at Candlestick Park, just as he had always wanted to do. It didn't matter that he was an usher, instead of a player. He was still here, still important. He had done what he set out to do.

And so had I.

Sunshine burned the fog away; flags fluttered over the center-field seats; a small airplane with an advertising streamer behind it flew across the blue sky beyond the stadium. I felt more alive than I ever had before, as if I could see and hear more clearly. I smelled the hot roasted peanuts; I felt the hard orange seat beneath me; I heard the sharp crack of the bat as it met the ball. *I will never*, I thought, *forget this afternoon*.

When the game ended, Dad stood at the bottom of the aisle, watching people leave. When our section was empty, he said, "I have to do what we call a 'clean sweep' before I leave. That means I walk up every row in my section, and gather what people left behind."

He let me help by walking the row next to his. We found an umbrella, a diaper bag, two seat cushions, and a purse—all of which Dad turned in to the Lost and Found. While we worked, he told me about one day when there was a minor earthquake during the ball game, and so many frightened fans rushed away that when the game ended, Dad found seventeen pairs of binoculars in his section!

Another day he found a wallet containing two hundred dollars. Every time I come with Dad, I decided, I will help him do the clean sweep.

We left the ballpark at Gate B because Dad had come by bus. Since he was an usher, he had arrived earlier than I had.

We took a different bus than the one I had come on. As we boarded, I planned to ask Dad to tell me more of the interesting things that had happened to him as an usher.

Instead, as soon as we were seated, he said, "It's great to see you, Spencer, and I want you to spend the night with me, but I'm afraid it won't work for you to live here."

I couldn't answer.

"I don't live alone," he said. "I share an apartment with my girlfriend, and we only have one bedroom. I'd like to have you stay with us, but it just isn't possible."

THIRTEEN

I stared down at my hands.

"You couldn't find my phone number," Dad said, "because the phone is in Sharon's name."

"I don't have anywhere else to go," I said. "I can't take Foxey back to Aunt May's. Cissy is allergic to him."

"Even if we had room for you to stay here, you wouldn't be able to keep the cat," he said. "Our landlord doesn't allow animals."

I wanted to ask, can't you move? Isn't your son important enough for that? But I already knew the answer.

"When we get home," Dad continued, "I'll call your

mother and tell her you're here. Then tomorrow, you can take the bus back to Seattle."

"What about Foxey?" I said.

"He can stay where he is. Let the guy who's taking care of him keep him."

I felt sick to my stomach.

I felt even sicker when I met Sharon. She listened to Dad's explanation of who I was and how I got there.

"So you ran away from home," she said to me. "What an idiotic thing to do. Where's your brain, boy? In the seat of your pants? Do you know how many perverts and thugs are on the streets?"

At least she didn't say ax murderers. As Sharon yammered on about how stupid I was, I knew Dad was right; it would never work for me to live with him, even if he wanted me. And the sad truth was, he didn't want me.

I took a much-needed shower and then Sharon and Dad ordered a pizza delivered for dinner. It was a pepperoni pizza. Dad doesn't know I am a vegetarian; Dad really doesn't know me at all. I picked off the meat and said nothing. I wasn't hungry, anyway.

Dad called the Greyhound station and found out what time the bus leaves for Seattle, and how much a ticket cost.

"We can't afford this," Sharon complained.

"Knock it off, Sharon," Dad said.

"I'll pay you back, after I get a job," I said.

"No," Dad said, glaring at Sharon. "You don't have to."

I felt a tiny bit better to have him stand up to her about the money. He must care for me a little, or he wouldn't bother to pay my way back to Seattle.

"Do you have May's phone number?" Dad asked.

"Yes."

"Do you want to talk to your mother, or do you want me to?"

"You can."

He dialed the number. "Hello, May," he said. "It's Jerome Atwood. Spencer is here with me."

He made a face and held the phone away from his ear; I could hear Aunt May screaming. Then Mama apparently got on the line, because Dad said, "Hello, Leona. Yes, he's here. He is fine. We're in San Francisco." There were brief pauses between each sentence, and I knew Mama was asking questions.

"He came alone," Dad said. "No, I didn't know he was coming, but I'm sending him back first thing tomorrow morning on the bus."

I listened as Dad told Mama when I would arrive. There was no regret in his voice, no hint that he was sorry I had to leave. He might have been making arrangements to ship a package via UPS.

After he hung up, he said, "Your mother will be there to meet the bus when it gets in."

Sharon started putting purple nail polish on her toes.

Dad asked me about school but there wasn't much to say. He asked again how I had managed to get to San Francisco by myself and this time I told him about sleeping in the park, and the boys who took my money, and about eating leftovers at McDonalds.

"Oh, gross!" Sharon said. "You should never eat a stranger's food. You could get AIDS."

I was glad when it was time to go to bed.

Dad gave me a blanket and pillow, and I slept on the living-room floor. I could hear him and Sharon talking in the bedroom, but I couldn't make out the words.

I stared at the ceiling. The idea of me and Dad living together, and going to watch the Giants play baseball, had been a wonderful dream. But in order for it to come true, Dad had to want me with him always, no matter what. The trouble with my dream was that I had to count on someone else to make it happen, and other people don't always act the way we want them to.

I realized that the Candlestick Park I had struggled to reach isn't a real place; it was only a ballpark in my mind, where everything was okay again. There is no more Candlestick Park; there is only 3COM Park. And I needed a new dream, something I could make happen by myself.

Early the next morning, Dad drove me back to the Transbay Transit Terminal building in downtown San Francisco. He didn't go in with me. He had to hurry back so Sharon could have the car to get to work. He stopped where the city buses and taxis stop, and handed me some money. "This is enough for your ticket and a couple of meals," he said.

"Thanks."

Dad got a funny look on his face. "It was good to see you, Spencer," he said. "I'll keep in touch."

I nodded, knowing he wouldn't.

I wanted to hug him, but that was awkward in the car. Dad put out his hand, and I shook it.

"Good-bye, Dad," I said. I jumped out of the car and hurried toward the door of the bus terminal. I looked back once, to wave, but Dad had already driven away.

I rode the escalators up to the Greyhound ticket counter. "Does the nine o'clock bus to Seattle stop at Grafton, Oregon?" I asked.

"No. It's an express run. The next bus to Grafton leaves at ten o'clock tonight."

I would have to wait around the bus station all day, but instead of buying a ticket to Seattle, I bought one for Grafton. Foxey and I would live with Hank.

The ticket to Grafton was less expensive than a ticket to Seattle, so I had extra money. I went back downstairs and across the street to a bagel shop. I bought two bagels, sat on a concrete bench in front of the terminal, and shared the bagels with a flock of pigeons.

When the bagels were gone, I walked to the Mosconi Center, and strolled around the gardens. I ate lunch, read a discarded newspaper, and sat on the grass by the waterfall, watching the other people.

I was glad I had left Foxey with Hank. The traffic noises—air brakes, horns honking, tires squealing—would have frightened him.

I saw a cluster of pay phones and thought about calling Hank, to tell him I was coming, but I decided not to waste the money. I knew Hank would be there, and I knew how to find him. Best of all, I knew Hank would be glad to see me. Hank *wanted* me to live with him; he wanted Foxey, too.

Funny. I felt more welcome with a man I barely knew than I did with my own father. And it would be a relief to live with someone who understands me.

Mama and I are different in so many ways, and I get the feeling she thinks the differences are my fault. Sometimes when Mama looks at me I know she is wondering how she produced a kid like me. She would probably think the hospital accidentally switched babies when I was born, except I look so much like Dad.

Well, it will be easier for Mama without me. I eat a lot, and I keep outgrowing my clothes. If I'm not there, Mama can work the dinner shift at Little Joe's. The tips are better then, but she usually worked days because she didn't like to leave me home alone after dark.

Maybe Mama will stay at Aunt May's; they are good company for each other and Mama gets along with Buzz and Cissy. Lots better than I do.

Eventually I would let Mama know where I was. Maybe I could even go visit her some time.

I returned to the Transit Terminal. While I waited, I made plans. Next week, I would go back to school. I wondered if there was more than one school in Grafton. Probably not. It isn't a very big town.

As soon as I got settled in school, I would look for a part-time job. I couldn't expect Hank to pay for everything, and I had to repay all the money listed in my debt journal.

Maybe I could get a paper route. If not, I would mow lawns or wash cars or baby-sit. Or maybe I could start a pet-care service. I could take care of people's dogs and cats when the people were not home and get paid for doing what I love to do.

By the time I finally boarded the bus, my head was full of plans and ideas.

As the bus drove away from San Francisco, I thought, Good-bye, Candlestick Park. It hurt to leave the dream behind, but I had a good new destination. Hank would be glad to see me; Foxey and I could stay together.

The bus ride soon lulled me to sleep, and I slept most of the time until morning. By then we were in Oregon, and I followed our progress on my map. The bus pulled up to the health food store in Grafton at two o'clock in the afternoon.

I smiled all the way to Hank's street, imagining his surprise and delight when he opened the door and saw me. And Foxey! I could hardly wait to nuzzle my nose into Foxey's thick fur and breathe in the special cat smell of him, and hear his happy purr.

I had left Foxey with Hank on Sunday and I returned to Grafton on Wednesday, but I felt as if half a lifetime had passed.

I trotted the last block, turned the corner, and stopped. Several cars were parked in front of Hank's house, and long tables containing household goods sat in Hank's front yard. A young couple came out of the house carrying Hank's radio, and a woman in a flowered dress emerged with her arms full of sheets and towels.

As I hurried closer, I saw a big yellow HOUSE FOR SALE sign in Hank's front yard. My smile vanished.

A man sat at a card table, collecting money for the items sold. Dread walked with me toward the man.

"What's going on?" I asked him.

"Estate sale," he replied. "Lots of bargains inside."

"Where's Hank?" I asked.

The man looked up. "Hank Woodworth died, three days ago. He had a heart attack Sunday afternoon. He managed to call 911, but when the ambulance got here, it was too late. He was already gone."

I stared at the man, not even trying to stop the tears that ran down my cheeks.

"I'm sorry, son," the man said. "I didn't realize you were a friend of Hank's."

"He was taking care of my cat for me," I said. Where was Foxey? The shock of Hank's death was pushed aside by fear. What had happened to Foxey?

The man abruptly stood up. "Byron!" he called. "The cat boy's here!"

A man in a business suit hurried over. "What's your name?" he asked.

"Spencer Atwood. Hank had my cat, Foxey. Do you know where he is?"

"I haven't been able to find the cat. I suspect he got spooked by the ambulance and all the commotion with the medics, and ran away. I'm Byron Mills, Hank Woodworth's attorney. He left a letter for you."

After the words, *ran away*, I barely heard the rest of what he said. Numb with grief, I took the business card he handed me and stuck it in my pocket.

Gone. Foxey was gone.

He's always been scared of loud noises. Whenever he heard a siren, he ran under the bed. Sometimes he stayed for hours, even when I tried to coax him out with a treat or his catnip mouse. He must have been terrified when the ambulance came, and the medics rushed in. In an emergency like that, nobody would notice if a cat got loose.

"Has anyone looked for him?" I asked.

"He isn't in the house, I'm sure of that," the card-table man said. "We went completely through yesterday, when we priced everything."

Hank was dead. Foxey was gone. I had lost my two best friends in the whole world, and I would have no choice now but to go back and live with Mama. I felt dizzy, and reached for the card table to steady myself.

"I think you need to sit down," Byron Mills said. "This has been a shock." He took my arm and led me to a white Lincoln that was parked just down the street. "Sit in here," he said, as he opened the door. "I'll bring you a drink of water."

I sat in the front seat, leaned my arms and head against the dashboard, and wept.

I should have stayed with Hank, I thought. If I had been here, I could have called for help sooner. The doctors might have been able to save Hank if they had more time. And I would have shut Foxey in my bedroom before the ambulance came. He would have been safe in there, hiding under my bed, and I would have been here to calm him down after they took Hank to the hospital.

I felt a hand on my shoulder. I took a deep breath, and looked up.

Mr. Mills held out a glass of water. He took a handkerchief out of his pocket and handed it to me.

I wiped my eyes and nose, and drank the water.

"There is business we need to talk about," Mr. Mills said. He got in the driver's seat and started the car.

"I'm going to take you to my office. Your letter from Hank is there, and I need to call your parents."

I didn't argue.

When we got to Mr. Mills's office, he opened a file cabinet and took out a white envelope. "Here's the letter," he said. "I opened it, since I did not know how to contact you."

I took the envelope. Across the front it said, "Spencer Atwood." There was a single sheet of notebook paper inside.

Dear Spencer:

A few hours after you left, I began having chest pains. They aren't too bad but I decided to put my affairs in order, just in case. I've rewritten my will. With Lois gone, and no children or other family, I had planned to leave everything to the Cat Rescue Society, where we adopted Butter. They will still get my house, but I've decided to leave my personal belongings and my savings to you. I want you to have some security so that you can afford to keep Foxey, whether you're with your dad or back with your mother.

Wherever you live, finish school, and then follow your dreams. You are a bright, kind boy, and I'm glad to be your friend.

Hank

I put the letter in my lap, and closed my eyes. Oh, Hank, I thought. I'm so sorry I didn't stay with you.

"Even though it is handwritten, the change he made to his will is legal," Byron Mills said. "He had two of his neighbors come over to witness his signature. I will manage your money in a trust fund until you're twenty-one, unless you need some for living expenses now or for college, if you choose to go."

Right then, I didn't care if I had inherited 10 million dollars. I just wanted Hank and Foxey back.

CHAPTER
FOURTEEN

I need your address and phone number," Mr. Mills said.

I wrote down Aunt May's address and phone number.

"It's my aunt's address," I said, as I gave it to him. "Mama's staying with her."

"And you live with them?"

I hesitated a moment. "Yes," I said. "That's where I live."

"I'll call your mother and make arrangements to get you home."

"Is it okay if I stay in Hank's house for a day or two?" I asked. "I want to try to find my cat."

Mr. Mills looked doubtful.

"Please?" I said. "I promise I won't leave."

"I'll have to make sure it's all right with your mother," he said. "Would she be at work now?"

"Wednesday's her day off."

Mr. Mills had a speaker phone in his office, and he explained that both of us could hear and talk.

Aunt May answered.

"This is Byron Mills, an attorney in Grafton, Oregon. Spencer Atwood is with me, and I'd like to speak to his mother, please."

It was no surprise to me when Aunt May started screaming, but Mr. Mills jumped about six inches.

"Spencer's in jail!" Aunt May hollered. "I knew it! I knew that boy would end up in trouble! He's in jail and some lawyer wants to talk to you!"

Mr. Mills turned down the volume on the speaker phone.

In the background, I heard Buzz and Cissy asking, "What did he do? What did he do? Did Spencer rob a bank?"

Finally Mama's voice, sounding scared, said, "Hello? This is Leona Atwood."

"Your son is not in trouble," Mr. Mills said.

"Is he all right?"

"Yes." Mr. Mills told Mama his name. "Spencer is with me," he continued, "because I represent the estate of Henry Woodworth, and Spencer was named in Henry's will."

There was a moment of silence. "Who's estate?" Mama said.

"You don't know him, Mama," I said. "He was a friend of mine."

"Mr. Woodworth has left your son some money and personal property here in Grafton," Mr. Mills said.

"An inheritance?" Mama said. She sounded incredulous, and Spencer smiled.

"The personal property is being sold," Mr. Mills said. "The proceeds will go into a trust fund for Spencer. I will administer the trust fund."

"How much money are you talking about?" Mama asked.

"Approximately twenty-five thousand dollars."

There was a clattering sound, as if Mama had dropped the telephone.

Aunt May screamed. Then she shouted into the telephone, "She's fainted! What did that boy do, to make his mama faint dead away on the floor?"

"When she comes to," Mr. Mills said, "tell her I'll call back later." He hung up.

"Do you see why I wanted to stay with Hank?" I said.

He laughed. "You and your mother will be able to have a place of your own now," he said.

He made a copy of Hank's letter and put it in the file. He smiled at me. "Since I didn't make arrangements for you to go home," he said, "I guess you'll have to stay at Hank's house tonight."

"Thanks."

"The sale goes until four o'clock today," Mr. Mills said. "We plan to hold another sale on Saturday. We'll have an ad in the paper for that one; today we just put out signs. In a small town like this, sometimes the signs are enough to draw a crowd."

I nodded. Mama often followed Yard Sale signs in Seattle, hoping to find bargains.

"If I had known you would show up so soon, I would have waited to have the sale, even though Hank's instructions said to do it immediately. There may be some things of Hank's that you want to keep."

"The cat carvings," I said. "He carved some cats out of wood; they were on the windowsill."

"You're in luck," Mr. Mills said. "We didn't put those in the sale because we wanted to have them appraised first. Most of Hank's belongings were ordinary used household items, but the wooden cats seemed to be authentic folk art. I have them at home; I'll see that you get them."

"Thanks," I said. I liked this man. I was glad Hank had chosen Mr. Mills to handle his affairs. And mine, I realized.

"Do you have any questions?"

"What happened to Hank?" I asked. "I mean, is he buried somewhere, or what?"

"His will requested immediate cremation, with the ashes to be scattered in the Cedar River. Those wishes were followed."

The tears filled my eyes again. I didn't say anything. What was there to say?

"Do you have any money?" Mr. Mills asked.

"Two dollars and sixty-five cents."

He took out his wallet and handed me a twenty-dollar bill. "Let me know if you need more," he said. "I put my home phone number on the card I gave you."

We drove back to Hank's house, and I sat in the car until four o'clock. I watched Mr. Mills's helpers carry the leftover sale items inside, and fold up the tables.

When they were ready to leave, Mr. Mills gave me a key to Hank's house. "I'm trusting you to stay here tonight, Spencer," he said, "because I trust Hank Woodworth's judgment. Let me know if you need anything, and call me in the morning."

"I will."

"I hope you find your cat."

I walked slowly into Hank's house. Much of the furniture was gone. The closet by the front door stood open; the closet was empty.

"Here, Foxey." I didn't think he was in the house, but I called anyway.

I went into Hank's bedroom; it contained only a stack of old *National Geographic* magazines. I went in the other bedroom, my bedroom. The dresser and chair were gone, but the bed was still there. I looked under the bed. No cat.

In the kitchen I found a half-full bowl of cat crunchies on the floor. A small saucer of water rested beside it.

I circled through the house twice, calling. When he didn't come, I went around the outside of the house.

Just because he didn't come didn't mean he wasn't there. Foxey has never come when I called him, unless he felt like coming. More than once, back in the old house, I walked through the yard calling and calling, only to discover him under a bush, watching me. It always made me laugh when Foxey did that because I knew he was behaving like a cat. But I never laughed until I found him, and I sure didn't feel like laughing now.

I looked in Hank's maple tree. I searched the old storage shed at the back of Hank's yard. I walked around the block, calling and looking.

When I didn't find him, I went downtown and bought two pieces of poster board, a wide black marker, and a roll of package tape.

As soon as I got back to Hank's house, I made LOST CAT signs. Hank's telephone had already been disconnected so I put his address on the signs. I also put "REWARD!!" I taped the signs to telephone poles, two blocks apart.

By then I was hungry. It was a shock to realize I could buy food without worrying about what it cost. Thank you, Hank, I thought, as I sat in the Corner Cafe, eating a big baked potato with cheese sauce.

It seemed odd, when I went back to the house, to

slip the key in the lock and let myself in. I wandered through the rooms for awhile. The TV was gone, and the bookshelves were empty.

I wondered where the bicycle was. I looked in the shed and around the yard, but it wasn't there. Probably it had already been sold. That gave me an idea.

I had been wondering how to make up for stealing the bike, since I didn't know who it belonged to or how to contact him. I decided the next time I saw a good bike at a yard sale, I would buy it with my lawn-mowing money and donate it to the Toys For Tots drive. That wouldn't help the boy whose bike I took, but it would get a bike to some kid who couldn't afford one. It was the best way I could think of to cancel my debt.

I unloaded the boxes of items that hadn't sold yet. At the bottom of the first box, I found a leash. I wondered if it had been Butter's, or if Hank had bought it for Foxey. I removed the price tag, and put the leash in my backpack.

After I went through all the boxes, I walked around the block again, looking for Foxey. Then I sat on the front porch steps. Every few minutes I called, "Here, Foxey!" just in case he was within earshot.

The sun set, the stars came out, and twice my chin dipped to my chest before I jerked awake again.

I did not want to go to bed. What if Foxey came back in the night and I didn't hear him? If I wasn't awake to let him in, he might run off again, and never return.

But the day's events had exhausted me. I dragged the mattress off the bed and pulled it into the living room, right beside the front door.

There was a chain lock on the inside of the door. With the chain fastened, I could open the door about four inches. That was plenty of room for Foxey to get inside. I put one of my shoes in the opening, to be sure the door didn't close. If Foxey came back and looked in the door, he would see me.

I lay on the mattress and thought about Hank, and about what Mr. Mills had said, that I could use Hank's money for college if I wanted to. I get good grades (except for the rat business in science) but I had never considered going to college, since I knew Mama could not afford to pay tuition.

Now it was different. Follow your dreams, Hank had written, and I planned to do what Hank suggested.

I vowed not to waste a penny of his money. I would make it last as long as possible and only pay for important things like rent. As soon as I was old enough, I would still get a part-time job, and maybe I really would go to college. Wouldn't that be something? No one in my family had ever done that before.

I began imagining signs:

Spencer's Pet Store

Spencer Atwood, Veterinarian
Spencer's Vegetarian Restaurant

No, I thought. If I ever own a restaurant, I'll call it Foxey's Place. Or Hank's Place. Or simply Hank's.

Still planning possible signs, I fell asleep.

I dreamed that I was trying to walk to Candlestick Park but I couldn't move my legs. I struggled and struggled, and finally woke up. I really couldn't move my legs—because Foxey was on top of me, stretched from my knees to my ankles.

I picked him up and hugged him. Foxey purred and rubbed his head against my shoulder. I put my face next to his, and he licked my cheek. I held him for a long time, and then I shut the door. I was determined never to lose Foxey again.

The next morning I went out for breakfast, and took down the LOST CAT signs.

At the pay phone by the drug store, I dialed the home number on Mr. Mills's card. Much as I wished Foxey and I could live alone in Hank's house, I knew it wasn't possible.

"I found my cat," I told Mr. Mills.

"I'm glad. Are you ready to go home?"

"Yes." What else could I do?

Home would not be near Candlestick Park, after all. It would probably be years before I saw another Giants game in person. Home wasn't going to be with Hank, either, who understood how I feel about animals because he loved them himself. Home was going to be with Mama, just like it's always been, and I wasn't at all sure she would let me keep Foxey, even if we moved out of Aunt May's house and into a place of our own.

"I'll come and get you," Mr. Mills said. "We can make travel plans from my office and then call your mother to let her know when to expect you. I'll take you and Foxey to the plane."

He said it casually, as if Foxey and I got on an airplane every day of our lives.

He arrived at Hank's house half an hour later and gave me a box containing all of Hank's wood carvings. I locked Hank's door, and handed the key to Mr. Mills.

We stopped downtown and bought a sturdy cat carrier that was small enough to fit under the seat of the plane. "That way Foxey can ride with you," Mr. Mills explained, "instead of with the cargo."

Foxey objected loudly to his new carrier, yowling all the way to Mr. Mills's office. We had to let him out in order for Mr. Mills to hear on the phone while he got my plane ticket and called Mama.

This time Mama didn't faint, even when he told her to pick me up at SeaTac Airport instead of the bus station. Maybe by now, nothing I do surprises Mama. All she said was, "I'll be glad to see him."

The flight was great, especially looking down at buildings that seemed like houses in a Monopoly game. Foxey's carrier had to be under the seat for take-off and landing, but the rest of the time the flight attendants said I could hold it in my lap. Once they let me open it and they all took a turn to pet Foxey.

They gave me little packs of peanuts and a Coke, and when we approached Seattle, I could see Mt. Rainier from above.

Only one thing marred the trip. I kept wondering what Mama would do when she saw Foxey. What if she said he had to go straight to Animal Control? I couldn't run away again; I had no place to go.

Maybe Mike's mother would let him have Foxey, and I could go to Mike's house to visit him. I blinked back tears at the idea of Foxey living with someone else, even Mike.

When I walked from the plane into the airport, Mama was waiting. I was glad she was alone. I didn't want to face Aunt May just yet, even though I had fourteen dollars folded together in my shirt pocket, all ready to give her.

Mama hugged me for a long time and I hugged back, surprised by how glad I was to see her. She looked at the cat carrier, but she didn't say anything about it and I didn't, either.

We went into the parking garage. "You got our car back!" I said.

"Mr. Mills called me again yesterday afternoon," Mama said. "He told me all about Hank Woodworth and explained how the trust fund will work. He also wired me money from the sale of Hank's household goods."

After we left the airport, we ordered milk shakes at

a Dairy Queen drive-through. Mama parked, and we sat in the car for almost an hour.

I expected Mama to yell for awhile, and tell me what my punishment was for running off and scaring her half to death. The worst punishment I could think of would be to give up Foxey.

Instead of yelling at me, Mama asked what had happened to me since I left Aunt May's. I told her everything and for once Mama listened and did not interrupt me. She smiled a little when I showed her my debt journal, but most of the time she looked sad and worried, especially when I told how the boys robbed me and about hitching a ride with the tattooed man and how I ate leftover food at McDonald's.

When I finished, she said, "You were wrong to leave, Spencer. A dozen disasters could have happened. What if Hank had lured you to his house by promising you cat food and then he turned out to be a maniac? That truck driver could have been an ax murderer. You are lucky to be alive instead of lying in a ditch somewhere."

"I know," I said. And I did know. Until Hank, no one I cared about had died. Mama's parents were killed in a car wreck when I was three but they lived in Florida, and I had never met them. At the time, I had wondered why Mama cried so hard.

Hank's death showed me how permanent death is. Hank is gone forever. Gone. I don't want my life to end for a long, long time so I won't hitchhike anymore, or ride a bike without a helmet, or go home with strangers.

"I won't run away again," I said. "I promise."

"I was wrong, too, Spencer," Mama said. "I know how much that fool cat means to you."

I clutched the cat carrier, daring to hope.

"After you left," Mama said, "I applied for a waitress job at The Courtyard. I start there next Monday. I'll get a dollar an hour more than at Little Joe's and the tips will be better."

"That's great, Mama," I said.

"I'm determined we won't ever be so desperate again."

"Do we still have to live with Aunt May?"

"Mr. Mills wired enough money to get the car back and to pay our back rent. Our old house was still vacant, so we're going there."

"Do I get to keep Foxey?"

"May says I'm out of my noggin to allow it, but yes, you can keep the cat."

"Thanks, Mama," I said.

Mama started the car.

I glanced over at her as she drove. She wasn't half as angry at me as I had expected. I wondered if Mama had once counted on Dad to make her dreams come true, just as I had, and it didn't happen for her, either. Maybe she knew how I felt. Maybe that's why she wasn't yelling at me.

"You look pretty today, Mama," I said.

"Don't try to butter me up, young man," Mama replied. "Just because I'm glad to see you doesn't mean you can weasel out of your chores."

I smiled, opened the cat carrier, and stroked Foxey's head. "We're going home now, Foxey," I told him. "We're going home."

Peg Kehret is the author of many popular novels for young readers, including *Cages*, *Danger at the Fair*, *Earthquake Terror*, *Horror at the Haunted House*, *Nightmare Mountain*, *Sisters Long Ago*, *Night of Fear*, *The Richest Kids in Town*, and *Terror at the Zoo*. Peg Kehret lives in Washington State with her husband.